Michael Gate

By Olga Yahontova

ISBN: 0615784712
ISBN 13: 9780615784717
Library of Congress Control Number: 2013905415

Cliffhouse Publications Incorporated
Santa Barbara, CA

To Andrei and Gabriel

Prologue

The rain rushed through the city with a hurricane, as a wolf unleashed from the deepest dark forest.

The pavement was shiny and clean under the light of a full moon, but the price of its cleansing was evidenced by fragments of broken tree branches and overturned garbage cans along the way. As he walked, he looked down at the rain-polished shoes carrying his steps through the empty city streets.

Nice.

The silence was almost absolute, the kind he liked best, with no signs of people, no cars, no apprehensive animal sounds, just the sweet taste of his own thoughts echoing visual images as he encountered them along the way. He tried the word *nice* again and it felt like sweet vanilla ice cream from his childhood. He liked remembering flavors through words that matched his feelings. It came naturally to him.

It was shortly before 6 a.m. and the city was asleep. He could sense people's breathing behind the stone walls of their homes. The wave was coming, he knew that already. He tried to cling to the taste of ice cream but the feeling melted, the anticipation washed it away, no trace of memory left.

His heart pounded, banging his chest from inside, not in a clinical way he had learned about in medical school, but from a power descending over him from above. No school had taught him about that.

He was more prepared now than he had been twenty-seven years ago when the power struck him for the first time. He knew now to let go of any fears, to let go of resistance, for they could damage him more than the unknown, and the unknown was the one calling for him.

He wouldn't remember much afterwards; in the past, especially in the first few years, he tried different tricks to consolidate his memory, determined to remember "the episodes." But all the tricks just brought more wounds and aches to his body, so he learned to let the memory go.

He wouldn't remember much of what happened to him in the hours to come. He would find himself in his home later on, before the sun rises, a sour, strange taste in his mouth, his body feeling alien, unknown. His sense of self would lurch like an old train pushing forward toward known and familiar ground, yet failing at every attempt to remember. Only one picture, a vivid dream, a beautiful hallucination, would linger in his consciousness — dark forest, a meadow with wild flowers, a white house lit by setting sun there in the middle. Again, this picture, so simple and tranquil and so painfully familiar, would hit him in the chest, taking his breath away with the weight of secrets and mystery. The sweet calling to remember will overwhelm him, pull tears from his tired eyes, but then the train will make a final push and he will remember himself again. As ever before, the picture will be suddenly forgotten, and he will go on with his familiar routine, happy and grateful to be back. But in the back of his mind, he will feel a lingering sadness, a sense of loss he can't quite define.

1.

Michael barely had time to suppress his yawn when the door shot open and a psych tech, a recently hired girl who was once a bodyguard for a Russian tycoon, brought in his next patient.

"Have a seat... Mr. Theodorus." Michael openly checked the name's spelling on the chart to make sure he was being transparent to his new patient, and in control of that transparency. He learned years ago that any attempt to pretend, hide, or bluff would leave him embarrassed and discontent. These were some of the smartest psychopaths ever caught and he had no chance to help them except to be better at their own game. Honesty was one of their main skills; they could take it, twist it, manipulate it. They felt entitled to own the naked truth along with everything else that came their way. They rarely lied because they didn't have to. They knew how to own people's emotions too, especially their insecurities. Michael had to discipline himself and work hard on his countertransference. The day he finally realized he was the one who had the key to this place — everything had changed.

"My name is Dr. Gate. Michael Gate. I am your new psychiatrist, Mr. Theodorus."

"Pleasure, Doc."

"I haven't had a chance to study your file yet. Do you want to tell me in your own words what brought you here?" Michael still felt sleepy from the previous night and had to squeeze his jaws to keep from yawning.

"Lisa did." The patient nodded toward the psych tech who was leaning casually against the wall, next to the door and the alarms. Theodorus was a man in his mid-forties, though Michael knew that most of the patients he saw looked younger than their biological age, unless drugs and excesses had worn them down. This one was disciplined, perfectly groomed, fit, awake, and self-confident. *He looks like John Malkovich*, Michael thought. He quickly tried to shake off this thought to avoid inviting the associations with the psychopaths played by the famous actor. *This one was going to be a handful.* Michael sensed it immediately.

The patient smiled politely as he continued answering Michael's question: "I don't mean to be a pain in your ass, Doc. I will cooperate. I just wanted to acknowledge Lisa, she is the sweetheart of this place."

He didn't have to try to be charming; he was natural at it, authenticity at its best.

Lisa was well-trained. They had paid her insane money, those paranoid Russians, so she could show up as their date at the party, be a cute, giggly, stupid blonde ready to seize any attack on her boss, whether it was a gun, a knife, martial arts, poison. Michael didn't understand why she would give up earning way more than what he was making as a doctor to work with the criminally insane.

"To keep it real," she had answered when he asked her, and he ended the conversation right there. The girl was a mystery, which for him meant trouble. Another lesson he learned long ago: never get involved with coworkers, no matter how cute they are.

She remained relaxed, leaning against the wall. Her caring facial expression had not changed a bit as the patient praised her.

"You seem to be a very perceptive psychiatrist, a smart one, a rarity behind these walls...." The patient started talking before Michael had a chance to ask his next question.

"Smart enough not to let flattery distract me." Michael felt an internal push to compose himself, to alert his attention above his usual vigilance. The man was dangerous; he oozed the sense of menace and ruthlessness of the crimes he had already committed and most likely still hoped to commit.

"Oh, no, I mean you're smart enough not to ask me about my mother and how she screwed up my pure little brain to make me such a horrible human being, you know, all your Freudian shit, because she was the sweetest lady and did no harm, just offered love, care, and unconditional support, like our little friend here." He nodded toward Lisa. She remained composed, attentive, and confident, just as the Russians trained her to be under stress.

"You are the one who is incarcerated, Mr. Theodorus, not your mother. Why don't we get back to what matters, and more specifically to what matters to me, and talk about you. I have quite a few questions."

"Shoot, Doc." The patient's eyes, light blue, deeply seated in his thin pale face, squeezed, and became intensely focused lenses that seemed to penetrate Michael's every cell. Theodorus straightened up in his chair, adopting a more alert, erect posture. "I mean, ask your questions, please, Doc."

The interview took about an hour and a half. Formal, required stream of questions followed by matter-of-fact, concise answers. Michael had no rapport with his new patient. He had to suppress his professional vanity not to fall into this challenge. He used to strive to make them emotional, to break them down, to attack their minds with the same ferocity and ruthlessness with which they had tormented their victims. This time his gut feeling — something he'd learned over the years to trust more than any sophisticated book knowledge — told him to shut down his striving for control and be as neutral as possible. His gut told him this choice might save his life. And even though that didn't make any logical sense — the patient was already locked up — Michael followed what the gut feeling instructed him to do. He remained neutral.

Although well aware of the risks, Michael hadn't been entirely truthful with his patient. He had looked through his chart, not as carefully as he would prefer but enough to know the story.

His controlling offense was a special allegation felony murder. From the police report:

The units were dispatched to an address on a report of a male subject who stated he had killed somebody and wanted someone to forgive him. Upon arrival at the scene, a force was required to open the door of the residence. The suspect was observed on the floor in the bedroom holding a metallic knife covered with what appeared to be blood in his hands. He became agitated when police arrived and refused to comply with the officer's commands. The suspect required three Taser applications before he was placed into handcuffs. While restrained on the floor the suspect addressed one of the officers with the question: "Do you know who is the true Messenger of the Gods?" Then he stated, "I am Him." Then he proceeded to sing loudly in an unrecognized language.

Michael watched his new patient carefully as he continued the interview. The man's appearance, relaxed and composed at the same time, could hardly indicate psychosis of that extent. Yet, he was described by previous evaluators as incapable of logical judgment and decision making. They had concluded that he certainly couldn't cooperate with his attorney in a clear and rational manner and that he was unable to respond appropriately to legal proceedings. The defendant met the criteria for the court to declare him incompetent, even though the evidence against him was circumstantial — his initial statement that he killed somebody, a bloody knife, and a few witnesses who recognized him as the man who got into a cab with the missing woman the night after the opera, almost a year ago.

Michael remembered that opera event, and the hype surrounding it, quite vividly. The opera itself was newsworthy, both for its subject matter and its performance, but the tragic disappearance of the director's girlfriend on opening night kept it in the mainstream and tabloid press for some time after.

It was late last November, in San Francisco. The opera premiere had been long awaited by many. *The Master and Margarita* was a story well known and beloved in many cultures outside its original Russian. Dark, twisted, mysterious, challenging, with satire and profound philosophy woven into a very personal and tragic love story, it was one of those books destined to become classic and stay in the collective mind for a long time.

The opera was the first successful attempt to create a performance based on *The Master and Margarita*. Great moviemakers and theater directors had dreamed of bringing the story to screen or stage and for one reason or another, all had failed. People flew from Europe and Russia for the first show and the excitement was all over the news. Michael had tried to get tickets, but the opera had sold out in less than an hour and he didn't feel like making an extra effort to find one. He had read the book long ago, barely skimming the surface of its social satire. The love story was touching but the characters, environment, the way of thinking was so foreign to Michael that he struggled to finish the book. Yet soon after, he dreamt of one of the book characters, a cat, the size of a human, walking on two feet and talking perfect English to him. The images from *The Master and Margarita* had entered his unconsciousness almost against his will.

The cat in Michael's dream was as sarcastic and playful as it was in the book. It wore a long grey coat, a hat, and leather gloves. Its unblinking cat's eyes were focused on Michael's face when it lifted its hat in a greeting and said gently and eloquently, "From one animal to another, Dr. Gate." Michael had awakened in a sweat. He decided then that the celebrated philosophy of *The Master and Margarita* was covertly related to Egyptian tradition. The talking cat reminded him of Egyptian Gods with animal heads. But unlike most, Michael, an avid reader of ancient mythology, always believed that those animal heads were actually masks covering human faces — a symbol for the next stage of human development. He even considered writing a paper for a Jungian journal on the symbolism of animal masks, but couldn't sustain enough interest in the subject to carry it on. And the feeling of unease from that cat dream had lingered, so he didn't regret not having opera tickets after all.

Michael remembered all this while looking through Theodorus' file and it awakened even more curiosity in the case. Michael realized that he had in his custody the one person who might have the answer to this mystery and now it was up to Michael and his skills to bring the answers into the light. He felt challenged and excited by this prospect.

The director's girlfriend was never found and one year later the case was still open. Very little was known about her. She had emigrated from Russia not long before her disappearance and worked as a translator. That's how she met the opera director, one of the most eligible bachelors in the country. There were rumors about her, mostly born out of jealousy. Many couldn't understand why the man desired by so many would choose someone so different, so aloof — a woman with a mysteriously tragic past. She didn't have friends, didn't seem to have any family, and when she disappeared the night after the opera, there was no relative to contact. Even her real name was a mystery — she had kept only her first name, Nadia, when she emigrated. Newspapers published her picture from one of the events she had attended and her striking looks — thin face framed by straight dark blonde hair, large, dark intense eyes full of deep sadness — added even more excitement to the mysterious disappearance. So far Theodorus was the only suspect.

Theodorus had stopped cooperating soon after his detention and talked only about his bizarre delusions of being the Messenger of the Gods and bold proclamations of "the end of the world as we know it." Michael could sense the frustration this man must have caused among detectives since they were likely ill-equipped to play the psychopath's mental games. He was certain they had pushed for incompetence so they wouldn't have to deal with him.

"Why did you scream and keep stripping yourself naked in jail, Mr. Theodorus?"

"So they would send me straight to your headquarters, Doc. It was simpler to arrange than I had expected. Police officers hear the word 'mental' and they go mental themselves. They will do anything to get rid of you if they think you're nuts. So they did."

Michael was not surprised by his new patient's bluntness. It was quite predictable. So he decided not to explore any of his patient's delusions and instead just ask about his history.

It appeared from Theodorus' self-report and was confirmed by available records that the last fifteen years Theodorus lived the life of a good, law-abiding citizen, after learning lessons from the time he served for previous offenses. He was under federal probation all these years, didn't have a single violation, and complied with all the requirements. His previous crimes included three forcible rapes, assault with a deadly weapon (knife), and drug-related charges.

Theodorus related his history in a dry, factual manner, and that was fine with Michael. He liked when his patients were well-educated about their legal cases, it made his job of information-gathering easier.

Michael collected his data in a matter-of-fact fashion, then he closed the chart, slipped his monogrammed pen into his pocket and signaled with a silent nod to Lisa that it was time for Theodorus to go. Lisa had been observing Theodorus' behavior silently and relentlessly and showed no signs of fatigue for having waited so long by the wall.

"Follow me, Mr. Theodorus, this way please." Her voice had no accent and sounded melodic and firm at the same time. The patient got up and followed her.

"So long, Dr. Gate," he said, making a short circular gesture with his right palm before leaving the office.

Michael remained silent and waited until the door clicked closed behind them. He rubbed his temples, his elbows resting on the desk. The early morning sleepiness was gone, but the heavy mental fog he had been fighting while interviewing Theodorus thickened — it was now a legitimate headache. Michael tried to brush it off, but changed his mind quickly; the headache was telling him something important.

His denial was a well-trained animal, domesticated years ago. It hardly had a power of its own. Michael believed himself in charge of his consciousness and all of its unconscious tools. He knew exactly who he was, had studied himself for years, as if his true self walked alongside his experience, documenting and analyzing everything while the other Michael, little Mike, walked headlong into trouble, got heartbroken over lost relationships, remained confused, angry, scared, and driven like most people.

Michael the observer learned from every bit of his experience, with no rest, no excuses, no false assumptions. He felt that self-study was his main obligation in life and he followed it diligently. Last year, he finally started reaping the rewards. It was almost as if the sage in him became realized, that the wise man who achieved ultimate mastery in life had finally came to understand the meaning of life. He still felt young, not just young at heart, but young in his fit, ripped, athletic body that he trained with the same diligence with which he trained his mind. He dressed well, casual enough for working in a prison hospital, yet stylish, confident, and modern.

He knew others thought of him as the best-looking doctor in the hospital and it fueled his vanity from time to time, but he was conscious of how temporary this was and never got attached to that sharp image he had created over the years. Deep down he knew he was flexible enough to take any form.

One of the benefits of his self-study was becoming a great forensic psychiatrist. Even his enemies (and there were quite a few who felt personally offended by or jealous of Michael's brilliance and charisma) agreed that he possessed the best clinical skills, intuition, and academic knowledge. He experienced a flush of joy dealing with the most dangerous emergency situations — riots, violence, malingering. Those moments were like entering a cage with a wild animal, enraged, apprehensive, ready to strike. In those moments he saw little difference between human and animal nature. He knew he had only a few seconds of pure instinctual, animalistic interaction with an enraged patient to reverse the situation — steady eye contact, carefully measured tone of voice and body posture all molded in one state of mind —with which he would envelop the patient, restrain him mentally, take away the force to fight, conforming him instead to his own will. It was all about energy. His staff found those moments irresistible, some called him a savior (he saved quite a few from really bad outcomes), some, a miracle worker. He preferred not to dwell on those moments. Patients loved him. Vicious gang bangers, thieves, rapists, pedophiles — especially broken and demented pedophiles — loved him and would never want another doctor. They felt his true compassion. He was among the very few who related to his patients with genuine respect. He was known to be fair and straightforward and he was never afraid of his patients. They were broken human beings, but they were human beings he understood well. His career was going smoothly.

Until today.

2.

The Opera House was a small building shaped like a perfect pyramid. An elaborate decoration of columns and ornaments surrounded the original structure in a freeform, asymmetric pattern. The lower part of the building was made of neatly arranged pale pink bricks. The upper part of the building was painted lemon yellow and even though the paint looked fresh and clean, as the building was relatively new, the combination of colors resulted in a worn and weathered look, creating an impression of an ancient, dream-like castle.

Nine Muses, surrounded by flowers, trees, and mythological characters, were depicted in bas-relief across the top of the building. Other figures were placed right above the entrance, between slender, off-white columns standing on either side of the main entrance. At the center was Mnemosyne, the Titan Goddess and the mother of the nine Muses, surrounded by two female figures and one winged male. They were realistic but not imposing. Few opera-goers paid attention to these decorations but unconsciously every visitor was touched by the power of the images as they prepared to cross the border into the land of art, the land of unknown... as they walked under the marble statues that seemed only pretending to be still.

Tonight the Opera House was filling up quickly with new guests as the clock's arm approached seven. A breath of cold air burst through the hall every time the doors opened to welcome crisp-dressed, fresh-faced women accompanied by reserved and uptight men. Perfumes, subtle and distinct, blended into a complex, singular scent that whispered *money* as guests wandered through the hall, talking in low voices to their company. The air of anticipation was building into an almost palpable intensity as if an invisible ether was altered by the desires and hopes of these men and women who had spent days waiting for this event, then hours preparing for tonight, only to finally be walking into their dream, ready to be changed forever. The strings in their imagination began to play the melody of change before the actual orchestra took their seats, before the light dimmed in heavy crystal chandeliers, before the rustling sounds became silence as everybody settled comfortably in the plush seats, mesmerized by tall, red, lavish curtains, waiting.

3.

There were times when Michael felt like a bullet shot from the barrel of a cosmic gun as an invisible finger pulled the trigger of his existence while somebody's squinted eye watched his explosion into this world.

Sometimes he felt enraged and compelled to turn around and scream into that squinted eye, "Why the fuck did you send me this way? What do you want me to do? Where am I supposed to go?"

And at each and every one of those moments, he had to remind himself that the bullet had no way of turning back, that his trajectory was determined by the size and the angle and the resolution of this primal pistol. In those moments he felt the speed of his flight and the resistance of the world and deep down he knew that when he hit the target it would be him who ended up dead as if he were a bullet aimed at its own mass, set for self- destruction.

The only comforting thought he got from this metaphor was that he never pictured that squinted eye laughing or indifferent or angry at him. It was always paying attention, always consumed by his trajectory and fully aware of the final target his life was supposed to hit.

This affected the way he related to people. He never shared the image with anybody, yet people, especially those who tried to get closer to him, sensed the bullet metaphor with their skin. Their nerves would fire up, making them anxious and scared around Michael. It was as if their instincts sniffed out the burning metal projectile and they knew it was only a matter of time before they would get hurt by him, no matter how kind, considerate, genuine, and caring he was in the moment.

Michael was a bullet and everybody else was passive material, an amorphous substance that would never be able to catch him or keep him or be close to him without experiencing the searing pain of abandonment. Most of the people who crossed his path left him before that point. Their instincts served them well. They left before the bullet hit them. And Michael remained lonely.

Michael didn't mind. It was the way he wanted it. His need for company, physical, sexual, intellectual — especially intellectual — was satisfied by selected, temporal encounters. His main companion was solitude and contrary to what most people would imagine, his solitude was overcrowded with thoughts, dialogues, images, memories, insights, and profound feelings that constituted more enjoyment than any external encounters ever could. Or had. He was the funniest person to be around for himself and inside his mind he had a blast.

Because people were not really a source of his pleasure, he never actively sought out their company. He didn't discriminate either, he was open to all of them equally, knowing from experience that communications he remembered best often came from unexpected sources; his criminally insane patients were the living proof of that. He learned more about life and human nature from their stories than from all the philosophy books he'd consumed earlier while searching for answers. The books were filled with somebody else's guesses, good ones at best, but most of them pompous and self-serving, no matter what culture, century, or school they came from. There was no substitute for real-life experience and for being able to perceive from another living being what her history and biology uncovered for her and to accept it as your own. Books were somebody's shadows, and as much as he loved playing with shadows, Michael always aimed for reality of his own light. That was his destination.

One thing Michael didn't know though, was that the reason he was lonely and isolated was because a being from another world had claimed his life long ago. So, as his psychiatrically trained mind continued to produce beautiful metaphors to explain his existence, his body lived a double life.

It started one day when Michael was eighteen years old.

He missed his class that day. It wasn't a planned absence, but the morning came early, shaking him up with its rough alarm sound. His body was still too relaxed after just a few hours of passing out that he felt he had no choice. The night before he'd attended a wild party; all new college students were partying like unleashed animals, like there was no tomorrow.

Michael pushed the alarm back to silence and made an instant decision to stay in his room and sleep. It wasn't a tough decision to make, and he didn't have to argue with himself, there was no guilt attached to missing school — he knew very well that he was capable and responsible and that one day of decent sleep wouldn't turn into a big problem.

He was wrong.

That day of sleep turned into the biggest kind of problem. That day turned Michael into somebody new, somebody he never dreamed of becoming. That day, his life course was altered for good.

As he slept, he dreamed that he was asleep on the grass under a big oak tree, hiding in its shadow from the afternoon heat. He felt like he wanted to wake up but sleep was still holding him tight in its magnetic womb, his body heavily plastered on the ground, his muscles relaxed and heavy at the same time.

He heard a bird twittering above his head. The sound of it was strange, harmonious yet alarming; it sounded almost like a child's voice had been hidden inside the melodious twittering. Michael didn't like it. He opened his eyes, squinted, and the next moment looked wide-eyed at his surroundings to see if it was really there. A small creature, a girl, dressed in something resembling a school uniform was hovering over him, her body held steadily in the air by a pair of extended wings fluttering quickly. She was laughing — it was her childlike laugh he had confused with the twittering. Her face was pretty, her body was half his size, and her age — she didn't seem to have an age. She stared directly into his eyes as she kept hovering in the same spot, her wings fluttering with rhythmic buzzing. She looked neither friendly, nor particularly hostile. Her laughter was not reflected on her face, her expression remained serious and maybe a little surprised. Michael understood then that she was not really laughing, she was communicating, and not with him.

He slowly sat up, still staring directly at her. Her wings buzzed louder for a second as she moved away from him. Michael cleared his throat but the question he was about to ask got stuck inside and he couldn't speak it. Somehow he found it embarrassing to address this creature and ask her, "What is your name?" Maybe it was her school uniform that made him nervous.

"My name is Maia," she said in a clear melodic voice and then laughed openly and loudly, this time laughing at him for sure.

"You think I'm funny?" Michael felt a certain bout of resentment.

"I find it funny that you think it is my dress that makes you nervous and you completely ignore my wings as if you see flying girls every day."

Michael knew she was right and didn't even think to question how she had read his thoughts, yet his resentment stayed.

"How about now?" She challenged him with a question and before he had time to realize what happened, she made a slight jerking move up and down and her body turned completely naked. It was a beautiful, fully formed, adult female body of perfect proportions flying right in front of his eyes and Michael felt that he was about to pass out.

"Feel better now?" She laughed.

Michael pushed his back against the tree trunk and froze there, shocked and mesmerized.

"Maia!" A commanding voice came from his right and he turned toward it with relief, as if looking for an anchor to save him from drowning in his confusion and embarrassment. But the sun was shining straight into his eyes and he couldn't see anybody. He blinked forcefully and tried to focus and then he recognized a figure approaching through the meadow.

Maia went through instantaneous transformation; her school uniform returned, her wings disappeared behind her back and she landed on the ground, her eyes down but her face still carrying a sly expression.

"I am sorry, Mistress, you know how humans are..."

"And how exactly are they?"

The voice got closer, and it was so full and powerful and familiar that Michael jumped on his feet and stood under the tree, waiting to see who was talking. His heart was about to jump out of his chest and the range of emotions that overpowered him was like nothing he had ever experienced. It was as if he were crying all the tears and experiencing all the pleasures at once. Her gait was strong, she was tall, almost his height, her hair was raven black and her skin porcelain. She wore a short tunic and tan sandals with tiny wings that were like small motors flickering around her ankles.

She walked toward him, and stood in front of his frozen body, her eyes directly in front of his eyes, and he felt like his world, as he knew it, had stopped. Not just for a moment in time, but for all time.

"Hello, Michael."

Her eyes were emerald green, and so unspeakably beautiful that nothing else mattered. He watched her in silence and he knew that he wanted this sight to last forever.

"That's exactly how they are. They create walls in their minds to shelter themselves from all of us and then act so stunned when they finally see — as if it wasn't them who placed those shades over their eyes in the first place. I mean, really, look at how shocked he acts, as if Mnemosyne had never visited him in his life." Maia sounded frustrated and Michael felt an urge to answer her and to tell her that he didn't pretend at all and that he really was shocked, but he couldn't turn away from these beautiful eyes looking at him with such warmth and understanding.

All he could do was force his mouth open to say, "Do I know you?"

"Here we go." Maia turned around and walked away as if she had enough of all this nonsense.

"You will."

As she spoke, Michael noticed how the tree greeted his guest. Its branches moved gently around her body, as if soothing and protecting her. Green leaves floated closer to her face, turning and playing with the light, and the substance of green diamonds that was visible inside the leaves sparkled and reflected in her eyes. Michael was convinced that some invisible energy flowed from the leaves' greenness into her eyes to make them so magical and mesmerizing. He couldn't say how long he stood there under the tree, in front of her, ecstatic and mesmerized.

The moment she touched his forehead with her long beautiful fingers sent a thunderstorm of understanding into every cell in Michael's body and soul. Instantly, the linear explanation of reality he was used to became unambiguously useless, limited, and unnecessary. Her divine nature became obvious through this touch too — Michael knew he was with the Goddess.

"My name is Artemis, Michael, and I've been waiting a long time for you," she said in her melodic voice which would send waves of pleasure through Michael's spine for years to come.

It was true what she said. Michael would never fully understand how Artemis had chosen him and she never discussed it with him. But Artemis had realized long ago that when the time came for her to fall in love with a human, it would be challenging and uneasy. She had been around humans for a long time and never before felt even the remote possibility that she might be in love with one. Until Michael came along. His sea-green eyes, his touching vulnerability, open and visible to her behind his sturdy physique, his shoulder-length dark brown hair, and his humbleness made him irresistible. He was different from all other humans she ever knew, he was modern and archaic simultaneously, and it was that paradox in particular that made her realize he was the One.

She knew Michael's questions before he formulated them and more importantly, she understood and released his fears before they took grip of his feelings. It was so nice and easy to be with her, she was everything Michael was looking for in a relationship and yet so much more.

"I want to stay here with you if I may." Michael felt shy yet his shyness didn't inhibit him.

Artemis smiled and touched Michael's long hair gently.

"You can. But it would involve some decisions on your part, my love." She said it so naturally, as if they had been a couple for a long time.

Michael listened intently.

"We Gods, like a pack of wolves, we run together in a way humans can't understand, unless they dive completely into their own animal nature, the way you would need to do, my love. Then and only then you can come back here and stay with me."

It made perfect sense for Michael; he saw nothing paradoxical in her statement, just a different kind of logic. He agreed to everything Artemis offered him. He didn't second-guess it at that moment and never after. It was so clear and straightforward in that reality with her that any linear question vanished, leaving him only with trust and awe.

For the first time in his life Michael felt that everything that happened to him was completely okay and he felt free. He knew that he would do anything she might ask of him. That was the first night they spent together, the first of many. Every time that followed he would remember everything that happened to him that night, every sweet sensation, joy, every movement and thought and feeling. Those things stayed with him, untouched, palpable, always available for him to remember in her presence.

He experienced transformation in his mind and in his body of such a proportion that if it had been somebody else, chances are they wouldn't survive it. Michael did. The challenge wasn't physical, it was existential in the most concrete sense of this world — deciding which direction his existence would shift, allowing this shift to happen, watching it happen, and still remain himself. It was like watching his personal universe collapse only to be reassembled once again from thousand of pieces of stardust into a shining new world.

Artemis was there guiding him, showing him the parts and dimensions of himself he would never before have guessed existed. But with her on his side everything was easy — she was the sun and the moon, and the ultimate magnet with a pull of such strength that he didn't have to choose anything — all he wanted was to follow her, and never stop.

He let go of his idea of himself, then let go of other people's ideas of him (a far more taxing task), and followed his primal unrestricted feelings, intoxicated with the joy from liberated instincts. He had become one hundred percent more himself, so much so that he knew he could choose any shape and form and that any of them still would be

Michael. He felt a particular inclination toward being a wolf. The energy, the character, and the disposition that came with a wolf's body made him feel the most at home. The wolf form was the glove that fit him best.

All of this, every memory from this first encounter was available to him, yet every time he experienced this place, this version of himself, the immediacy of the present experience was so consuming that he never had a chance to ponder those memories. Instead, the memories had become him, and without them he wouldn't be able to feel and experience his presence here in the same way. It was so different from the way his mind and his memories interacted in his human reality. Here he could see how limited his human mind was in experiencing the totality of past and present, but there was nothing he could do to take this knowledge with him.

The amnesia between worlds wasn't planned. Artemis would have been happy for him to remember everything. She was surprised when she realized Michael had no memory of her upon his return to his daily life. He didn't plan it either. His conditioning had such a strong hold on his human mind that each time the transformation back to human was complete, Michael lost all the memories of being with Artemis in this magical reality. The deep hurt he perceived every time waking up after an "episode" didn't come from the bruises, it was the pain from disconnected memories.

But he didn't know.

4.

The group session was scheduled for just after lunch, so it usually took Michael a few minutes to get everybody's attention. He would typically make a few jokes or ask some personal questions so he could command his patients' attention before proceeding.

The group's official name was "Stage Treatment," a product of a cognitive-behavioral approach developed specifically to reform the sex offender's mind. Michael had been using this approach for years. Part of the process had become a mechanical repetition for him, yet only a small part, for most of his group sessions were defined by un-predictable interactions with his patients' minds as he attempted to unlock the mystery of evil. He had accepted that he was dealing with evil, even though such concepts in general were too black and white for his refined mind. At the very beginning of his work as an SVP (Sexually Violent Predators) psychiatrist he had to sort through his own feelings and reactions toward the stories he would read in their charts and hear from their lips — and it wasn't easy. In fact, it was so difficult that one day after a month of trying to stay neutral and therapeutic while reading and hearing about child kidnapping, rape, torture, hunting, and rituals he did something unthinkable.

It happened in one of his early groups. He was guiding one of the child molesters who started talking about his crimes for the first time.

The patient did not start with the account of the actual kidnappings of three little boys and not with all the tricks and preparation he used to arrange it. He, for some reason, began his account with the present, sharing what was on his mind at that very moment.

He said to his peers: "I heard some of you saying in this group how you miss the rush of your crimes, how you try to go back there in your memory to get that feeling. I relate to this craving. I know it well. But my memory was never enough to satisfy it. It only made the craving more unbearable when I tried to recall and retain all the small details of what I did to those boys. It drove me nuts the first few years here, the thought of being locked up and never being able to touch another child again. There were times when I thought about doing away with myself, it was that bad. And then one day, I was laying in my bed, alone in my cell, half asleep, and a miracle happened. Honestly, it was almost like somebody guided me in my sleep through my own mind. My mind was this dark room and it had steps downstairs and I walked down and felt everything as if it was real, I felt it with my skin, with my very bones, and here it was — a perfect dungeon, a place in my mind that no one can ever find, and that nobody can ever take away from me. It was different from a dream, it was as real as hallucination, but it wasn't scary at all. I was ready to use it, all right. From that point on it was so easy for me to go there and to bring my boys with me. The place is magic, I tell you, it makes everything you see so real. At first they cry, then they get hungry, then they obey whatever I tell them to do just to get a little food. They are always there in my imagination, ready for me to come and play with them, and nobody can take these boys away from me."

Michael saw how his patient became more and more excited as he kept talking. He was getting off to these images and he didn't even try to hide it. Michael suddenly couldn't breathe, his heart was pounding, his palms sweating, he felt like he was witnessing something happening in real time, in this place — innocent little boys were locked up inside this monster's mind and he kept torturing them and there was nothing anybody could do to stop it. It was that real. The next thing Michael knew, he had stood abruptly, stared straight into his patient's eyes, and said, "And I want to share with you what I feel right now, and what I would like to do more than anything."

Everybody in the group got silent, waiting for Michael to continue. None of his patients had ever seen him this intense. He was almost shaking.

"What I would like to do is to jump on this table and stab you with a knife, drive it through your heart and tear your eyes out with my bare hands, so your mind is stopped and those children are set free."

Michael thought that he was crying, his face felt wet, but it was just precipitation from the intense emotions that overwhelmed him. A stunning silence hung in the room with his patients. Rapists and child molesters sat around the table looking at their doctor, who had just crashed in his chair and covered his face, unable to look at any one of them. The silence lingered, but somehow it wasn't uncomfortable, it felt necessary.

Then one of his patients said calmly, "It's okay, Doc, we understand."

Michael looked around the room and saw their faces. Nobody looked angry, but somehow they looked real, raw and real in a new way Michael hadn't seen before. He felt at that moment that they accepted him on a deeper level than he could have hoped for. Only now he was becoming their therapist.

"That's why I can tell you stuff like that, Doc, because of the way you are. You understand," the patient who told his story said. He added, "Because I want to be free from it, too."

After that group, Michael started to feel like he was moving with his patients somehow. They were tiny steps, and the paths weren't easy or clear, but something had changed. It was as if a glimpse of hope had entered the room that day and everybody in the group felt it.

Michael thought it was his openly expressed aggression that had helped his patients open up, but the feeling of hope was coming from something else that nobody in the group, including Michael, consciously realized. It was coming from the fact that they all had witnessed the power of the invisible world that lies beyond imagination. For one moment that afternoon, they experienced the reality of other dimensions as real as their daily lives, and the feeling of mystery and endless possibilities, good and bad, had touched them all.

But Michael didn't see it this way for a long time, and he preferred not to dwell on that experience.

On this day, nearly 14 years later, the group was almost over when a loud siren suddenly burst into the room, interrupting his speech. Michael's response was instinctual. He stood, told his patients that he had to stop the group, then ran toward the siren, which sounded too close, meaning that the trouble was next door in the middle of his unit. He had no time to waste. He remembered to nod to the technician who was assigned to his group to let all the patients out of the room and lock the door. The protocol for safety was to be followed precisely. It wasn't a bureaucratic demand but a survival code for everybody working here. Things could go wrong in a second and a seemingly peaceful day could turn into a life and death situation in the blink of an eye.

The day room where patients watched TV, played games, and held ward government meetings was already filled with cops; the hospital had its own police and the officers were well-trained for emergencies. They gave way to Michael the moment they saw him, recognizing that he was the boss who was supposed to restore order. The cops trusted him, having observed how in previous crisis situations he never failed to stay cool and take care of dangerous patients.

Michael's attention was super-focused. He walked through the room straight to the center of the brawl. His patient was lying on the floor face down, his body pinned by cops and staff. They were already placing restraints on his legs and hands as he kept spitting and cussing.

"Hi, David, Dr. Gate is here." Michael recognized him right away — a young, cocky guy who had just come from prison and was having a hard time giving up the prison mentality he was so proud of.

"Gate my ass, motherfucker!" The patient tried to turn his head and spit at Michael. That was enough for Michael to determine that David was actually okay, he was still enraged and fighting, yet alert, oriented, and physically intact. As he walked through the room to give orders for emergency medications, the nurse briefed Michael on the situation. They had picked up David in the main yard where he was trading cigarettes. Cigarettes, which were prohibited in the hospital, were running up to $20 a piece, a profitable business on a hospital's black market.

"David followed staff instructions at first and came back to the unit, and then he suddenly lost it and started attacking everybody. It took quite a few bodies to restrain him, we have one staff down," the nurse reported.

Michael looked around and saw that the floor, walls, and windows in the nursing station were stained with red blood and realized that it wasn't David's, that somebody on his team had gotten hurt pretty badly. His heart jumped into his throat.

"Who?"

"Lisa." The nurse nodded her head toward the nursing station. Michael couldn't see her at first — people were surrounding from all sides, taking care of her. Michael moved slowly, following a blood trace that became thicker and darker as he approached her.

Lisa was half-lying in a chair, her head tilted back, the right side of her face and eye swollen, her long blonde hair soaked in blood. She was breathing rapidly, irregularly, and she was crying. An older nurse was washing her face with a white cloth, cleaning off blood as they were preparing to stitch up her wounds. Michael felt relieved, realizing that her wounds must be bloody but superficial, something that could be taken care of here, otherwise she would already have been on her way to an outside hospital. But his relief was mixed with anxiety; something very deep inside of him was troubled in an unusual way. He felt vulnerable and emotional for the first time in many, many years.

"Here, sweetheart, you look beautiful again," the nurse said to Lisa as she finished cleaning her face. Her voice was gentle, calming yet firm, she knew well how to take care of her patients.

Lisa's response was unexpected; she burst into sobs, grabbed the nurse's hand, and whispered, "Don't leave me, Maria, don't leave me please."

"You are not that lucky, sweetheart, not today, I ain't going anywhere. I still have to sew up your pretty face." Maria laughed gently as she removed herself from Lisa's grasp and opened a suturing kit.

"I thought you were one tough cookie, sweetheart," she said gently as she daubed Lisa's face with an alcohol swab. Lisa stopped crying but her breathing remained heavy, distressed. There was silence in the room for a while. Maria started to place the sutures, her hands moving professionally and gently to minimize Lisa's pain. Yet it was obvious for Michael that it wasn't the physical pain Lisa was responding to. She could tolerate much more physical discomfort, and she wasn't afraid either. Something else had broken her, something Michael didn't understand. Yet.

"You know, Maria, when a woman dies inside for money, she becomes much worse a monster than a man can ever be."

Michael perked up at this, curious about the seemingly random statement. But perhaps it wasn't random at all.

"Sweetheart, normally I would tell you to shut your pretty mouth tight when I am working on your face, but you are an exceptional girl, and you need to talk, what can I do?" Maria's voice sounded cheerful and encouraging. She knew so well after years spent in the hospital how to make her patients talk. "Why did you let him do it to you, then?" Maria asked, ignoring Lisa's statement. "I saw the incident. He punched you and threw you against the wall like a doll, and you didn't move a finger to protect yourself. Yet when he was about to attack another staff member who rushed to help you, you jumped him in a second. You took him down before anybody had time to react, even when you were bleeding all over the place. It was like in a movie or something, very impressive. So why did you let him do it to you in the first place, sweetheart? You have to tell me now so I don't have any bad dreams tonight."

"So I can feel something..."

"When was it that you stopped feeling?"

"When I started working for this woman..."

"The one who died inside for money?"

"Yea, that one. Ouch!" Lisa made a jerking movement in the chair as the needle entered her skin near her eyelid.

Lisa couldn't see Michael; her chair was strategically turned away from the door and from the large, heavy, crack-proof windows. Michael stepped in front of her and spoke.

"I am so sorry, Lisa. I know you can't talk right now, but when Maria is done I would like to talk to you for a few moments, just to debrief what happened."

Lisa nodded and her eyes lit with something that looked like relief when she saw Michael. His protective presence had always brought reassurance, but there was something else in her eyes, something that reminded him of a little girl in trouble who finally sees her dad coming to save her.

Well... anybody regresses when in pain, Michael thought.

When Maria was finally done, having placed a perfect last stitch on Lisa's now clean but slightly swollen face, Michael took over. He led Lisa to his office, closed the door and sat facing her, ready to begin. He had done this many times, too many, debriefing staff after an attack on the unit to make sure no aspect of trauma stayed unattended only to return later as relentless nightmares, anxieties, or sometimes as drugs and alcohol. Lisa was ready to talk, she looked more open and vulnerable than ever, and Michael knew it would only take a small push to release her story.

"Who did you lose back in Russia?"

She looked at him in disbelief, her cool façade gone, her entire face screaming, "How do you know?"

There was no need to explain. It was one of the standard questions from the debriefing protocol to identify previous traumas, and since most of her life had been in Russia, he had just used logic to frame the question. Michael also knew that a little air of mystery could give him greater access to her psyche — people share their secrets more willingly while facing enigma in another — the copying mechanism. Michael waited in silence.

"I had a teacher.... He was a friend of my father and after my dad started drinking a lot, this Teacher took me into his school and started training me. I was ten years old then. He taught me what is called internal martial arts, mostly Ba Gua. Our daily routine was very strict, we studied and practiced for hours and I loved every second of my life then. I didn't really know my biological parents — my mother died when I was young and though my father's body was still around, his spirit had gone far away where I couldn't find him. All I had was my Teacher. He was my mother and my father. He raised me against the world."

"What do you mean 'against the world'?"

"He taught me to live by internal rules, not by the social rules the world imposes. My Teacher protected me from TV, from common education. He raised me to believe that I was special and beautiful.

I grew up sheltered from cruelty, greed, from ugly things. He had substantial means, my Teacher; I think it was a large inheritance. And he never hesitated to spend it so 'his kids,' as he called me and two other boys in the school, had everything we needed. It was like a fairytale, it was so easy to learn and practice, and we became very advanced in our techniques and abilities.

"He was very pure, my Teacher, not naïve, but pure in the way he refused to let this world of people touch him. He wasn't lonely, yet he was alone often. There was this air of solitude around him that only one person seemed to be able to break."

She paused.

"There was a woman who visited him in school once in a while, and I knew they were in love just from the way they looked at each other. Her name was Nadia. We didn't like her much. I admit we were jealous — after all, she was able to reach him in ways none of us could. We knew he loved us, he took great care of us. But he loved her more than us, he loved her more than he loved himself. He became almost kid-like when she showed up to visit. She didn't care about us at all. The moment she appeared at the school door, with her long leather gloves, gorgeous coats — so beautiful yet remote as a star — all she wanted was to be with him. She was nice to us, but as if through a fog. She never remembered our names, all she saw was him. I think she was married or something. I don't know why they never moved in together — nobody would ask him about it. Clearly this woman was somebody special, almost sacred to him. He revered her, adored her, and at the end it was enough for us to see our Teacher happy, so we finally accepted her — or at least what she represented to him.

"He was practical, fair, straightforward and unbelievably strong in his art. He was the best Ba Gua practitioner of our time, I have no doubt, yet he had no vanity. He never wanted the prizes or recognition and fame he could have easily enjoyed."

Lisa shifted in her seat a bit, settled into it as though relaxing ever so slightly.

"'Whatever your need is,' he used to tell me, 'the help and support for it will always find their way to you. Don't beg other people for anything; there is nothing they can give you that you don't already have.'

"I trusted him with my life. And I would have given my life for him in a second. I didn't get that chance. He was taken from us without warning. The police officers showed up at the school — we had started living there soon after our training began — and somebody kept crying, 'It was a car accident!' People were running around like crazy. My mind separated into two parts, one listening to and following what people around me were telling me to do, and the other one knowing as deeply as knowing can ever be that my Teacher was gone. I never learned the details of what happened. Some of his friends believed his rivals arranged the accident, others rejected the conspiracy theories and just accepted that he died instantly in a car crash. I did neither.

"They moved us out a few days later, the school property was sealed, and I had to go back to live with my biological father in his small studio apartment. I was seventeen and had one more year before I could live independently. I lost my brothers, the two boys I grew up with in the school, as they were returned to their families far away. In the chaos that had erupted, we never had a chance even to talk to each other.

"This is when the hell of my life began. Not just because I missed the Ba Gua community, but mostly because I felt that I was losing myself to the world. Everything my Teacher taught me about the world and its people seemed too lofty, as I suddenly found myself in a smelly, dark, unbearable apartment, thinking about how to survive. They put me in a public school. I went there once and never went back. I had no plans, no friends, no material means to live on in this world. When they disconnected the electricity in the apartment because my father spent his monthly retirement on cheap vodka, I knew better than to ask him for anything. I just walked out to the street, repeating to myself my Teacher's words, that help and support will always find their way to me. Little did I know just what that 'help and support' would look like...."

Lisa closed her eyes and sighed deeply. Michael sat in front of her, attentive and compassionate. She hadn't reached the end of her story, yet it was already predictable as if some bad screenwriter had outlined the drama, and it bothered him deeply, bothered him to the bone. A burning question appeared on top of the crisis experience:

What the hell had happened that this girl, so well trained and composed, started to fall apart now? Why did she choose this moment to open the wounds that she was able to bury for such a long time? Michael sensed that the answer to this question was vitally important to him, because the same force that had broken down Lisa's defenses was coming after him. That was what bothered him the most, even though he didn't yet realize it.

"Look at me, just spilling my guts to you. I... I should stop..." she began.

Michael opened his mouth to encourage her, to give her permission to continue, but he didn't have to say a word.

Lisa sighed, then started up again. "To finish my story, there was a fight at the subway station, and I got involved because somebody pushed me really hard and my instincts clicked. A wealthy man saw me fighting, took me aside, invited me to his BMW and there it was — my first job sealed. I worked as his bodyguard for a few months, and then he sold his business, a telephone company, to a new owner. I was a part of the business, so I got moved as well. My new boss was a woman and she was evil in the truest meaning of this word. And worst of all, she knew it. She was aware and proud of what she had become, her ruthlessness and coldness were her best investments. She believed she had achieved not only external power over the poor people working for her, but internal power as well. She thought she was cool. But all she was — was prematurely dead. And that was pathetic.

"I watched her interact with her family. She was divorced and had a six-year-old son, who she'd already trained as a tool for her revenge. One dead woman can create many future bad boys, you know. Her mother was an old, wheelchair-bound wreck and even though she never had much to say I often felt that her slouched, crippled body hid the mind and the story that were the original source of all the evil in this family, and that she knew it, but felt nothing about it.

"My boss hired young prostitutes often, mostly underage girls who were happy to please her in order to make enough money to buy food and clothes. I had to stop feeling; they were all monsters....

"Some say Dostoyevsky's reality came back to Russia. Not so much. In his books, his heroes realized that they were suffering, but there was hope behind the darkness in his pages. The people of today don't have any self-reflection — they eat, drink, have sex, collect payments, they don't know suffering, they have anxieties. One can only hope that Dostoyevsky's reality comes back to his land.

"One day, I learned that my boss had arranged an explosion in a children's theater, to eliminate her rival who was attending a Christmas show with her granddaughter. When I learned about it, I had to warn that woman. So I had to leave. And besides my existential disgust, I had to save my ass too, because my boss would never let me live after what I had done. I had to get myself as far away as possible, which is right here on our hospital grounds. Good thing I had saved most of the money they paid me and had my passport and US visa ready in advance."

"That's it?" She was hiding something, a secret, that he felt would make sense to her entire story. The story without the secret had no real flesh to it but felt instead like a constructed narrative.

"Pretty much." Lisa's face was more swollen and red now, her eyes looked sleepy and Michael wondered if they had given her Valium before sewing the stitches. "What else do you want to know?"

Michael paused one more second and then it dawned on him, the key came floating to him in his mind in large blue letters spelling a word, a name in his inner vision. That name was the key to all the missing pieces of her story.

"What happened to Nadia?" he asked as casually as possible.

"Nadia disappeared too, nobody saw her since. I think she went overseas or something."

If Michael had any doubts, her response erased them. Her face became flushed, pupils jumped into large dark holes, her breathing accelerated, and she squeezed the chair arms tightly. Her ability to play cool and to hide her emotions was certainly diminished by the trauma she just had experienced.

This was the sort of moment in his professional life Michael loved the most — the moment when he was about to uncover a hidden piece that made sense out of the entire story. The puzzle pieces shifted, moved as if driven by the magnet of the secret and the entire picture emerged — complex, dynamic, alive. Nadia was the key, the answer to why this girl ended up in this God-forgotten place, far away from home. Michael had no doubt that the woman from Lisa's story, her teacher's love, was the same Nadia from Theodorus' file, the victim of the kidnapping case. Not just because her name, description, and nationality were identical, but mostly because his instinct told him it was the same woman, the one he never met, yet she was already unmistakably recognizable to him as if she had imprinted herself in his consciousness.

He decided not to push Lisa too hard, after all she had just experienced a serious trauma.

"You followed Nadia, right, this is why you ended up here?"

She looked at him almost with horror, the same *how did you know?* shock stamped on her face while she remained silent, speechless.

"I know, Lisa, and now you know that I know. Just tell me why you did, you will feel better."

One moment of heavy silence and then the dam burst. Her hands squeezed the chair until her knuckles turned pale, she clenched her teeth, and the deeply seated fire came to the surface of her huge pupils as she burst into tirade.

"Because I never trusted her! Because I wanted to prove that she was a fake, I wanted to expose her for who she really was even after he was gone, even after! Yes, you got it right! It mattered to me to bring her to light, she was not the woman he thought he loved, she was ordinary, average, pretending to be somebody special. She pretended well, oh yes she did! She was even able to trick my Teacher so he fell for her the same way all the others did. She was a fox, a psychopath, cold and empty and full of herself, but I saw through her arrogance, through her aloof shell of a being. She didn't love him. Not even a little! That love between them, it wasn't real, it was all his imagination. We were his family!"

Michael was thankful they'd given her Valium. He backed away instinctively as the small Russian girl looked much more dangerous and scary than most of his agitated patients.

"I see you have very strong feelings for this woman. What were you able to find out about her?"

This was a moment that Michael called "the gift of the day." This is how he named those instances when on top of information he was looking for in his interactions, something else surfaced, something spontaneous and unexpected that brought him insight and understanding he didn't expect. Every time it felt like Christmas. And he felt like a chess player and a hunter at the same time and they were both winning.

Lisa was obviously unaware of Theodorus' suspicious connection to Nadia, the legal information was usually a privilege for clinical staff only, and yet she had become a source of information about the life of this woman before her disappearance, information that could be invaluable in cracking the case.

"I found out enough to dismiss her from my memory, for good. I don't want to be mean, and I know it would sound horrible, but she deserved what happened to her."

"What happened?"

"She disappeared. Without any trace. But knowing her well now, I would bet that it was her own decision, that somehow she got what she wanted and got away with that."

"What do you think she wanted?"

"I don't know for sure, but I do know that whatever this woman wanted she always got. Even before she was gone she was able to seduce a famous director, Raphael Storm. Did you know he created the whole opera for her? Well, she took it all for granted of course and then disappeared in the thin air right on the night of the premiere. The woman was malicious." Lisa sounded calmer now, it was relaxing and liberating for her to finally share something that she kept building up in secret for a long time.

"How long has it been since your teacher was killed?"

"A few years, why?"

"Because you seem to judge a woman for not staying faithful to somebody who died. Yet after a few years, isn't it normal to move on?"

"So now you are protecting her too?" She sounded sarcastic for the first time since Michael knew her.

"No, I am trying to help you see the source of your pain."

Lisa didn't say anything. She looked in agony and pensive at the same time, and Michael suddenly knew precisely how to release her from her pain. But it had to wait a little longer. He needed to get more information about Nadia.

"Tell me how did you find her here."

"I worked in private security in Russia, remember? It is the easiest thing to do to track somebody down. I made a few phone calls, spent some dollars, and soon her entire record was on my laptop. I knew that she immigrated officially, that she had changed her last name after she finalized her divorce. She got her interpreter's license and was doing some freelance work. She rented a small cottage on the beach; she clearly had same savings because she lived comfortably. And she ceased all her connections with Russia. None of her friends knew where she went and she didn't make new friends here. I think she started writing because that's what she was doing most of her free time until she met Raphael Storm."

"How did they meet?"

"At work. She was hired to translate for him. The Mikhail Bulgakov novel, you know it?" Lisa caught Michael's observant look and laughed, for the first time during this conversation. "No, I wasn't following her then, I just know it from their conversations afterwards. They met at work, quite predictably. He'd always been surrounded by beautiful girls craving his attention, but she was the one who caught his because she was avoiding everybody and pushing him away until he made her change her mind and give him a chance. Pretty clever."

"You are saying it as if it was Nadia's strategy to get him. Do you really believe that?"

"No, I don't think she did it consciously..."

"Well, you can't speak with certainty for her unconsciousness either, Lisa. And I think this is a source of your pain."

"What?"

"The fact that you let yourself believe something that had no grounds only because it appealed to your anger. You distorted reality to fit your idea of it and that distortion is the main cause of pain."

"I am not sure I follow you."

"I will explain. Why didn't you protect yourself today when the patient attacked you?"

She remained silent.

"I will help you. Because you felt that you deserved the punishment, am I right?"

She lowered her head as if unwillingly agreeing.

"Do you know why you feel you deserve the punishment?"

Lisa looked up at Michael, tears building in her eyes, and said softly, "I don't know."

"I believe you, and I am going to help you because I think I know precisely why you did it. You did it because you feel that you betrayed your Teacher... wait, don't rush, don't dismiss what I am saying, just stay with me here and listen to your feelings — they will tell you if what I am saying is true. You feel that you betrayed your Teacher and the reason for it is different from what your mind may come up with right now, very different. Deep down you know that what you did with Nadia is not okay. No matter how hard you try to justify it, you know that he wouldn't approve. You created an opinion about this woman whom your teacher loved and you went very far to prove it right, too far. It is not your place to judge their relationship; it is not your place to protect his memory. You betrayed your teacher by treating the woman he loved unfairly. That is why you tried to punish yourself."

She remained silent.

"Well it worked, here you are in pain and we are talking about it. It's okay to let it go now, because you are going to go home and take time off to heal and I am going to give you the name of a very good friend of mine who is the best therapist in town and she will help you to get through this. You can learn from this experience and start moving in the direction where the main source of your anger lies — in your relationship with your mother and in your anger at her for leaving you so early."

"You are too much." Lisa looked at Michael, shaking her head as if in disbelief.

"None of us is too much. Life sometimes is too much but nothing that you can't deal with. Really, as Maria said, you are one tough cookie, Lisa."

She smiled and took the therapist's phone number. He could see that she felt much better already, and he felt good about it, too. But before she was gone, one burning question remained, the one that had bothered him from the very beginning.

"Why today?"

"What?"

"What happened today that you let your guard down? Why?"

"It was your new patient, that guy with the long hair, what's his name? I was walking through the hall and passed by him, right before David went off, when he whispered, 'Break it down.' It was so subtle, yet it went into my mind like a snake. I felt his whisper physically touching me and then everything exploded. I think he pushed something purposefully in my subconscious, and you know what, it's okay."

Lisa looked at Michael. A barely noticeable half smile returned to her face, covering up the traces of recent tears. She looked confident again, relieved and relaxed, as if a spring storm went through her being and cleaned up all of last year's garbage.

"I feel good now. I realize that I confused peace of mind with numbness. Things are clearer now. I can see everything the way my Teacher would see it."

Lisa got up to leave. The nurse was waiting outside to walk her to her car. Michael let her go as his own mind prepared for the next task. He wasn't going to waste any time. He had to find his new patient, Theodorus. He knew already it wouldn't be pretty.

5.

The lights faded away as the sound gradually overtook the senses. It came from far away, as a muffled thunder at first, lingering for a while next to a disappearing light, half-full in its acoustic strength, not quite music yet, competing for the audience's perception until it overwhelmed their vision with the force of a primordial animal roaring in the darkness.

The overture had started.

As Raphael made his way through the concert hall, carefully in the darkness, a melody ruptured through the multitude of thundering sounds and made its fluid way through the space. It was the sound of flute and violin intertwined with almost mathematical precision, and it came from above, from the center of the crystal chandelier far from the orchestra. All other sounds faded away so the melody could have its way, uninterrupted, on its journey to the deepest layer of the human soul, where love had not been felt before. The melody was a boat carrying love directly to the people in the audience, and they had no clue what was about to touch them.

Raphael smiled as he took his aisle seat. He knew what was about to happen. He was the creator of the show and was pleased to see how it began unfolding. It was the first public performance. All bets were off and the stakes were high, but he felt confident, relaxed, and hopeful because he knew it would work as it was supposed to.

Nobody seemed to notice that the fine melody was coming from the center of the ceiling. "People have gotten used to technology, we should use it freely in our opera. It would not take anything away from the performance, it would only enhance the magic," Raphael had argued with the sound designer.

The curtain moved, first slowly, and then swiftly, casually. The scene looked casual too. The mostly empty urban street, dim light tinted with a grey-blue to create a sensation of rain, and a small figure of a woman frozen on the edge, stopped in a moment just before making her first steps on stage. The only bright spot in the scene was a bouquet of yellow flowers in her hands. Everything else in her silhouette remained dark, hidden in the shadow, undetermined yet.

The music, as counterpoint to the mystery on the stage, announced itself in a mighty river, cascading from the multitude of instruments skillfully played by the orchestra. The melody, carried from the ceiling, left no doubt for the audience that this story was about love, because nothing else mattered and the woman on stage knew it so well, for so long, as she made her first step toward the audience, the first careful step, holding her flowers as if her life depended on them.

She started singing. Raphael closed his eyes to focus on her voice, and even though he knew it so well, every time it touched him as if hearing her for the first time.

He knew the script, deeper than by heart, he knew it personally, with a degree of jealousy that only great men can experience — a sense of sorrow from lacking something that was not supposed to come his way. To facilitate it in the world, to tell the story in a new form was the only way he had to touch it. And at this moment he felt nothing but gratitude for being allowed to bring them back, the Master and Margarita, to make them visible and known and alive once again before love took them away. Love was the main character in this story and she was fierce and omnipotent.

Margarita sang in a deep voice, more common for a rock performance than for opera. Her voice matched the melody perfectly and the song was full of such sorrow and hopelessness that the audience froze. All eyes were transfixed on her small figure: black coat, yellow flowers. She sang that her life was full of great things, except for love, and that she refused to continue living without it. If she didn't meet him today, so be it, she asked fate to let her go, for an existence without love was unbearable.

The melody followed her words, as if listening to her song and confirming that it was indeed her story, and she was as connected with the music as the music was with her.

The intimacy of the scene was palpable. Raphael couldn't see the audience's reaction, but he could feel it strongly — the miracle of many strangers connecting, merging, sharing emotions, becoming one breathing body, woven by voice and music into one shared feeling.

He knew Nadia was part of it tonight, the woman who mattered so much, the one he wanted to bring happiness and healing, helping her forget her loss. *The Master and Margarita* was her favorite book and he had labored to bring it to stage, just for her. He wasn't sure she was aware of her role, but she was here tonight, in the front row, the premiere ticket he secured for her long ago. That much was certain.

She was dressed in a silver evening swing coat cut just above her knees, a little side of a black dress visible beneath it, her beautiful legs in sheer stockings exposed and those striking blue shoes with thick high heels and little golden hearts with diamonds dangling on the sides, a bold statement very few women could pull off. Nadia had a natural sense of style and she was always a magnet for social attention. Raphael felt somewhat disappointed that she had chosen to attend the premiere alone. He certainly would have felt proud to have her by his side. But... she was watching and she was listening and he could feel it. *Help her forget her sorrow, Gods ...if she can.*

On stage, a male figure parted from the dark wall, tall, slim, dressed in a long coat. His part was as much physical as it was vocal. His few steps approaching the woman had been rehearsed a million times — each step one piece of a perfect metaphor for the fateful determination of their story. It was their first meeting, the lovers coming together for the first time, but their moving silhouettes were already filled with knowledge of what was to come.

Raphael had auditioned two choreographers before he found Mark, a young man fresh from dance school who was able to create plasticity and magic through the characters' movements just the way Raphael had envisioned. It was minimalistic, just two silhouettes, male and female moving toward each other, but their eyes were locked, their hands trembling slightly, their bodies almost restrained from running toward each other. Small steps, yet inevitable. The effect worked, the audience could feel their anticipation with an entire range of emotions. They fell into an art-induced trance, connecting the images on the stage with emotional memories from their own lives, each so unique yet similar to the couple on stage.

He closed his eyes again and tried to imagine what Nadia must be feeling. He could picture her image clearly as she sat in her privileged, front row seat, mesmerized, waiting for magic to begin, waiting for *The Master and Margarita* to come alive.

In quiet defiance of the strict Soviet rule, Bulgakov's novel had become a gate to freedom to believe. It was a gate to the supernatural, where the black and white restrictions of traditional religion were challenged by raw and complex honesty of human nature. Raphael knew that for Nadia it had always been a story of redeemed love, finding the one you lost, even before she had experienced the multiplied pain of her own loss.

As the music continued and Margarita sang, he pictured the little girl in Nadia who wanted to believe in magic, imagined her grow stronger and more present until her whole being gave herself to the music, washing away all the doubts and confirming the reality of magic as solid and as indisputable as the Opera House around her. He could almost sense the images from her childhood she once shared rising up in her mind. The music, the silhouettes, the illusion of rain on stage bringing forgotten associations from her childhood Siberian winters. Surely she would see a snow-covered playground, a lonely crow jumping awkwardly through the empty ground picking up pieces of last year grass from under the snow. Surely she would remember the feeling of solitude acutely as she had once looked through the window at the snow-covered silent landscape, her forehead pressed against the cold glass, freezing, her dark eyes fixed on the figure of the black bird contrasted against the white snow. Surely her mind would accept the conviction that she would do anything to break this solitude and find a person in her life to love and to feel close to.

Raphael sensed — no, he knew — all her memories, brought to the surface by strange associations with the opera, were mixing with her immediate perception so the performance was becoming her memory. This story was becoming her story and he was glad he was able to do this for her. All for her. He hoped it would help her to heal and turn to him so he could take care of her.

He couldn't have been further from the truth.

Nadia closed her eyes to deny the tears welling up under her long thick lashes, then signed deeply. When she opened her eyes, she felt relaxed and resolved. At the very moment when Margarita threw away the yellow flowers before falling into the embrace of her beloved, Nadia knew with adamant certainty that her time had come.

6.

Michael moved quickly. He had a mission now. He found Theodorus sitting in a corner of the day room, all by himself watching other patients in silence. He stood up the moment he saw Michael.

"Can I talk to you now, Mr. Theodorus?" Michael's voice was calm and inviting. Theodorus smiled slightly as he followed Michael into his office.

"Have a seat, please." Michael's demeanor was courteous, but his insides seethed.

"I see you're angry, Doc."

"And I see you are still doing what you do best — reading people's minds. Should I order you a daily newspaper, Mr. Theodorus, so you have something else to read?"

"It is nice of you, Doc, but sarcasm aside, there is nothing in world affairs that can surprise me. So thank you, no. How can I help you?"

"You are not here to help me, or for that matter, anybody else, Mr. Theodorus, remember? You are here to get help for yourself. So let's focus on how I can help *you* today." Michael was tired of fighting his emotions toward this man. He was about to call for what it really was, the evilness in his nature that wasn't a result of illness. A pure and straightforward evil, self-sufficient and self-sustained. No more need for excuses, at least on his side.

Michael knew he didn't have to like his patient. Still, he had this eerie feeling that his patient was more aware than he was of what was about to come. Theodorus looked calm and composed and completely relaxed. He sat in front of Michael's desk, watching him with patience and with what Michael perceived to be an almost perverse understanding. Yet, his eyes were mutilating, as if they had invisible rays coming from the very center of his dark pupils, penetrating Michael's flesh, going through his nerves, cutting all the connections that his body and mind knew as their own, down to the very essence of his soul. They were mutilating what he knew about himself, without remorse, without compassion, just a pure surgical excision of his essence. Michael had to shake his head to remain focused.

"How is our friend Lisa?" Theodorus wasn't even trying to hide his game.

Michael had to pause for a moment so his voice wouldn't reveal his outrage.

"Lisa is not your friend. You know that. This is about you. Tell me, Mr. Theodorus, do you consider yourself one of the Gods?" Michael kept his tone as neutral as possible.

"As a thorough psychiatrist, which you are, Mr. Gate, you should have studied my file by now and you would know that the answer to your question is no. No, I do not consider myself one of the Gods, Mr. Gate." It bothered Michael that Theodorus was calling him Mister instead of Doctor, but it wasn't time to pay attention to that. Not yet.

"I consider myself one of their messengers," Theodorus continued.

Michael began to nod, an automatic professional gesture that stated wordlessly, *keep talking, I am listening.*

"Humans are very arrogant beings, you know." Theodorus spoke in a soft low voice; there was something hypnotizing in the rhythm and intonation of his speech.

"That is quite a generalization," Michael commented.

"No. It is a literality of self-obsessed and ridiculously narrowed human entitlement. Have you noticed, that they, I mean humans, apply the definition of evil to anything that threatens to break their denial?"

"Well, just an observation — you are one of the most entitled people I've ever met, Mr. Theodorus." Michael wasn't sure where this dialogue was going, but he started feeling calmer; he switched from rage to an awakening interest. Theodorus sounded more open than at their first meeting and Michael didn't want to miss his chance for discovery.

"So I speak from experience," Theodorus said, offering a wry smile. "The only difference between me and people you've met, Mr. Gate, is that I have a whole range of other experiences that don't allow me to identify with this human entitlement. I know more than that."

"Because you're a messenger of the Gods."

"Definitely." Theodorus was ignoring Michael's sarcasm as if it was an inevitable childish reaction. "That and many other experiences."

"Like what?"

"Simple ones, like going to the zoo and watching giraffes, for example."

"Giraffes? Why giraffes?"

"Because they are one of the most transcendent and sensitive creatures under this sky. Whenever I see them, I always feel that they belong to different dimensions, their feet are on the ground, but their necks are breaking through tangible matter, almost like a bamboo tree would break through concrete, so their eyes can see realities invisible to others. They're not afraid to belong to both worlds.

"But what is more relevant for our conversation is not the mere existence of these beautiful creatures, but rather the principle of divine analogy that I was exercising while talking about them, the same way I did when I compared Lisa to my mother at our first meeting — I have a good memory, Mr. Gate, I am sure you do, too. You see, when I did that I didn't project her onto my mother, or my mother onto her, as any stupid shrink —not you, of course — would think. But I associated my denial with Lisa's. I made an analogy and it wasn't a coincidence. I had experienced a lot of denial about my mother. She was a cold, psychotic, and jealous bitch who never knew how to be a mother. You see, it's not as much about the content of what we say as it is about the form. The old philosophical dilemma, resolved by me long ago. Successfully, I must add. The form always prevails, content is irrelevant when it comes to influencing people's minds. So you connect with people's defenses first, using the analogy principle, intentionally, and then break them up in yourself and people will follow.

"When you truly connect to people they will follow you anywhere, they will dive off the abyss if the analogy you have made for them is correct. It is very simple. Yes, the mechanics of manipulating people's minds can be used to harm. But it can also save. That's why I call it divine. In Lisa's case, I used it to help her break through. I helped her."

Despite all the multitude of responses queuing up in his mind, Michael forced himself to remain silent, to listen.

"So going back to your original question," Theodorus continued, "being a messenger of the Gods doesn't make me more special than any other human being. It is just a result of me becoming more aware of my own nature, something any human can do if he chooses to raise his awareness."

"So everybody is a messenger of the Gods?"

"No, but everybody has a range of other extraordinary experiences they choose to forget so their limited perception of reality remains intact."

"I see..."

"No, you don't. You don't see it, because if you did, you wouldn't have felt enraged today when Lisa experienced something that was returned to her. It was her choice and her experience and it is going to be good for her. Yet you felt anger instead. And then that anger blinded you and you directed it toward me. Your anger is a shield, Mr. Gate, an emotional filter that keeps your memories and feelings unchartered. So is the arrogance you're feeling right now. Don't you feel uneasy, Mr. Gate, thinking how dare I analyze you? You, the one who has the key to this place! How dare I speak to you as if I knew something more than you do, you, an established, brilliant professional, an expert in the field of human drives and desires?"

Michael smiled and didn't say anything. Theodorus was right, those thoughts did indeed flash through his mind. And those thoughts, Michael had to admit, were damn right arrogant. So he kept listening.

"You have trained your arrogance, often masking it as humility, so you can allow yourself to be humble when you have all the control. You think you can let the chaos of this place unravel as much as it can, because you are in control, since you have the key. True.

"But you forget one thing, Mr. Gate. When you leave this place with your key chained to your belt, you are not as safe as you would like to think. You take a deeper, less known and more dangerous chaos with you: the one that's settled inside your soul. You don't have the key to lock that up, do you? How are you going to control that?"

Theodorus sniffled and wiped his nose with the back of his hand, a gesture so starkly in contrast to the composed, thoughtful analysis he presented, it startled Michael. Theodorus didn't seem to notice, or care. He continued on as if there had been no pause at all.

"You know why you work out so much? Somebody less insightful might say — oh, it's because he is insecure, he wants to be attractive, it's a 'macho' thing, and the whole mid-life crisis bullshit. I, on the other hand, am insightful enough, Mr. Gate, to know that your impressive physique is further evidence of your incredible sensitivity. By buffing up your muscles you enforce your boundaries, the physical boundaries of your physical body, and by the amount of work you obviously put into your muscles I must conclude that somehow, somewhere those very boundaries of yours have been challenged and maybe even violated. How is that for an analysis?"

Michael didn't move a muscle. He knew Theodorus hadn't finished yet.

"There is more. You think you love your job because of the humanity of it. There is some truth in this, but that's not the primary reason. Every time you see straps tightened up across somebody's chest as they are being restrained you feel satisfaction that more madness, more violence, more rage is being restrained and contained so everybody in this world is a little safer. This, too, is true, but there is more. Every time you witness this scene, you patch up a wall in your mind — a wall that divides your experience, a wall that confirms you are safe because everything prohibited, inappropriate, dangerous is under control and locked away from this reality. But not only madness and rage and violence are being locked up — so also are immense beauty, magic, love beyond belief, and miraculous possibilities. Your fear tricks you and locks these away as well, keeping them hidden behind the straps you put on your consciousness. The result? Your memory is divided and your soul suffers."

"Wow, Mr. Theodorus, that is quite a dramatic statement. So you suggest I stop restraining any agitated, raging patient from now on?"

"I suggest that you let yourself loose in your own so-called un-consciousness, Mr. Gate. It can be a lot of fun, actually." Theodorus again swiped his arm across his nose. It was such a juvenile gesture. Raw and unrefined. Then he continued, "By the way, when I attached my denial to Lisa's, you were there in the room. So was your denial. Maybe that is why you feel so uneasy?"

Michael kept his mouth shut, waiting. A short pause followed and then Theodorus spoke, in a somewhat tired voice.

"I have a deal for you, Mr. Gate." Then he paused again. "I will help you experience your own return and I will ask you something in exchange."

"Return of what?"

"Return of what you have locked up behind your inner walls, re-turn of something that you are longing for so much but can't allow yourself to remember. I will help you find where you left the keys."

"And if I was supposedly interested, what would you want in exchange?"

"I will tell you in a moment." Mr. Theodorus got silent again and watched Michael with a long, sustained pause that somehow wasn't uncomfortable. Michael didn't mind playing this game; he was finally getting information.

"Death is a privilege, Mr. Gate."

That was random, Michael thought. He said, "How do I know that it is not your defense talking now? And how would you know that your statement is not serving to pacify your guilt and fears, Mr. Theodorus, assuming you have some?"

"Because I had a choice, a choice to kill. As much as she had a choice to die. There is nothing to defend. Defense is a burp-up game of unresolved conflict, of unfinished choice. My choice was complete before I acted upon it, Mr. Gate."

"Can you please call me Doctor Gate?"

"I will when you become one."

Michael felt a sudden rush of rage, followed by a nano-second of self-analysis that gave him pause. He hadn't realized that his profes-sional pride was so strong before he heard this statement. He chose not to respond and instead just kept looking at his patient silently and attentively.

"You see now, like at any other time, there is no need for you to feel angry. I told the truth. Souls don't compete. People's personalities do. To be more precise, the programs that run people's minds compete, trying to make sure that the illusions they create are stronger than the competing ones. Psychiatry is notorious for playing with this subtle programming. Because, you see, there is this trick, this assumption that having a medical degree, being a psychiatrist, somehow gives a 'doctor' an access to understanding, a right to judge other people's souls as if they understood their own. They pretend to be equipped to interfere in the matters of human souls, often without remembering who they are themselves. That's why I told you the very first day that you are a rarity behind these walls. You have compassion and you are humble, and you have a genuine need to know yourself, and you worked hard on getting to know yourself. And you want to heal the suffering souls.

"I can't call you the doctor yet because you don't know more than I do about the shadow side of yourself and therefore you don't have a choice when it's time for that side to act out. I do. I am more advanced. Still..." he paused. Michael waited for the nose-wiping gesture, but it didn't come. "Still... I need your help." His gaze was heavy and full of so much sadness.

"And what do you think I can help you with?" Strangely, Michael's anger was gone. For the first time in this conversation he didn't feel a need to compete. This was a new sense, liberating and comforting at the same time. Theodorus looked at him intently. Michael could physically sense the heaviness of his gaze.

Theodorus stared directly into his eyes for a moment before answering: "To achieve the privilege of my death, Mr. Gate."

7.

He knew in his animal shape that the planet beneath his paws was spherical, he knew it through the way he had to push, to propel his body to run through the thick layer of grey grass reflecting the full moon with drops of budding dew. The earth and the moon mirrored each other through his body stretched in his run in between them, pushed by their mutual gravity toward his only destination.

Her.

Being with Artemis gave Michael the greatest sense of completeness he had never known. It was as if she filled up all the gaps in his psyche — gaps that ached every time she was away. The gaps were different in his mind as a wolf and in his mind as a human. He was more aware and complete in his animal shape, yet the transformation that turned him into a wolf, and back, served as a wall, an invisible, yet inflexible barrier between him and Michael, the man. And while he preserved his human memory after the transformation, something else stayed behind — a sense of identity.

In his animal shape Michael knew he'd left behind a lonely, confused psychiatrist, but he didn't have access to his own self that refused to remember him. That was a loss. A painful loss. At times Michael the man felt a wave of excitement as if he had a premonition that something really good was about to happen, something magical, miraculous, something that would change his life completely. He felt elated and liberated in those moments. The anticipation of a miracle was like a little drug that made him high. But those moments were short-lived. His rational thinking would inevitably take over and burst the bubble with a razor of reason edged with cynicism. And suddenly, the magic would be gone. The wall prevailed.

So every moment in the forest was precious. Even though Michael always remembered a bitter taste of separation that the wall had created, he made every effort to live the moments with her to the fullest.

He saw her and recognized her immediately, recognized with a full memory that hit so deeply he had to gasp for air. The memory grabbed him by his throat and threw him in the midst of a hot, magical, unbelievable dream. The reality of the dream stuck to his very skin, crawled under it, and all the cells in his body were shaken and his entire awareness crushed into a new, but so sweetly familiar memory of her. She laughed. Her laughter was beautiful and sweet; it went down Michael's spine as a stream of crystal water and refreshed everything in his body.

"Every time you go through it, my love, every time. And every time I find it so cute."

He stood up firmly and shook his body, feeling a wave of incredible strength flow to his muscles. He smiled and looked back at her, fully realizing his power.

"Here we go, my love, come back." She spun and started running through the meadow, the little pink wings around her ankles flickering with gold. Her feet barely touched the ground, yet her run was strong. Michael jumped and pushed himself to follow her. He felt the forgotten joy of stretching those sinewy muscles, the joy from recognizing patterns of his wolf body that were under his full control. He raced after her, breathing deeply with his ribs, sensing all the flowery smells of the ground beneath him, following her lithe and weightless figure as his guide in this universe of magic. He followed her path without looking, his head down, his eyes on the ground, unfocused, yet his run through the forest was precise, certain.

He was used to going through the transformation. The first few years were the toughest, but it became almost instantaneous. He knew the mechanism well. The only part of becoming a wolf that still kept him fascinated was the flood of returned memory — he retained all his knowledge from his life as a human but along with his wolf's body he gained a whole universe of other memories and instincts.

The running instinct was one of the strongest. Michael, the man, was a highly visual person — the impressive art collection he gathered over the years was a testimony to this. Years of working with the criminally insane conditioned him to watch his back, literally, the hospital was littered with half-circle wall mirrors. When he was a wolf running through the forest, vision was a secondary sense, images didn't matter. Scent did, above all, hearing was a close second, but scent was his navigator. He perceived it geometrically. The subtle changes of layers of scents created the reality for him, and he knew exactly how to move through it. If he followed his vision, everything would slow down. Smells gave him speed, immediate perception, and direct knowledge of this reality.

The wolf in him would smile from time to time, remembering how limited his perception was as a celebrated psychiatrist and how naïve and arrogant he was in his human form, thinking that he had the keys to understanding reality. But those were rare instances; he didn't like reflecting on that other reality. The "lesser one," he called it. His time here was limited, by what, he wasn't quite sure, and he wanted to experience it in full, without distraction.

Michael pushed his body through the tall grass with large strides, forcefully and freely, the joy of a liberated body present in him more than ever. He sensed Artemis, smelled her, only occasionally glimpsing a golden flicker of her sandals' wings. He breathed evenly, his mind was calm, his soul at peace — he was ready for whatever surprise she had in store for him.

Then suddenly the ground under him ended, and he found himself hurtling over a cliff's edge. The only thing he perceived before his body plunged into the abyss was Artemis' melodic laughter, sweet and gentle, washing away Michael's fears as it always did. His body flew through the air, propelled by the energy of the run. His blood pulsed intently in accordance with a new rhythm he didn't understand yet, while his body already followed it, holding itself up in the air while something inside unlocked and forced elaborate, wide, and powerful wings to spread from his sides. The wind caught him, and Michael navigated his way in the air streams. His instincts changed, he was in human form again, only larger and winged. The space before him was open, with no separation between earth and sky. He was in the middle and belonged to both. He tasted the joy of flying for the first time. He heard Artemis speak directly into his mind.

"Shape is omnipotent, yet irrelevant. Learning to switch is the key to eternity. Enjoy reshaping, my love."

"So you can keep me as your lover forever?"

"You bet."

8.

The bruise hurt beyond its physical boundaries. It appeared as just a small spot on the left leg but managed to send shocks of pain far, at some turns all the way to the groin. Michael moaned instinctively every time he made a wrong move. He could never get used to the bruises, but he was troubled more by the fact that he couldn't explain his episodes — that some part of his experience was separated from his conscious awareness. Deep down, he associated the mystery with shame and secrecy, shame that prevented him from exploring the episodes. He didn't dare look more closely at what was happening, certain such an investigation would challenge his entire understanding, pushing his self-knowledge to a test he never felt ready to take.

No matter where the episodes struck Michael, he always woke up from them in the comfort of his own home. He found it quite convenient; at least there was a small part of these experiences that felt predictable and safe. Besides, whenever he returned he was starving like an animal. He learned early on to always make sure his refrigerator was stocked with good food — frozen gourmet meals, a carton of fresh milk and tons of chicken (fried, barbequed, marinated, grilled with all kinds of exotic sauces). Chicken never tasted better to

Michael than after an episode. It was as if tasting it for the very first time.

His house was a bachelor's dream. A flat screen TV occupied an entire wall, perfect for watching football games while lying on the comfortable, stylish sofa, drinking beer. The glass doors to the garden were gigantic, the ceiling was huge and the whole place was lit brilliantly throughout every season.

No matter how late it might make him to work, Michael always found time to step out to the garden before leaving his house. It was one of his rituals, a moment of silence and self-reflection that kept him sane before stepping into the reality of the criminally insane, no matter what he had to face.

This morning was no exception. Despite the pain from the bruise, Michael walked into his garden, a cup of freshly made coffee in his hand. The garden was wild and by someone else's standards might have been considered uncared for. But Michael had never paid attention to other people's standards. His garden was his life and every single plant, tree, every little spring on the ground were attended with utmost attention. There were no strangers in his garden, ever. Michael's privacy reached its height when it came to this space and the only creatures he would share his garden with were occasional birds coming to visit and to taste the sweet syrup Michael left for them in a feeder.

The feeder was an old ceramic plate with intricate edges in the form of different fruits hanging on a short chain from a large tree branch. Michael bought it from his favorite antique store. The store was called the Antique Mall — a strange warehouse with the yard usually full of junk. It was a 30 minute drive to this store that seemed to grow up out of nowhere and in the middle of nowhere, perfectly situated between two towns. Every time he drove there was an adventure. He never actually knew if the store would be open or if Clarice, the store owner for the last 35 years, had decided to take a day off, locked everything up and headed off on one of her treasure hunts, probably in the southwest. But if the store was open, Clarice would be sitting in her antique rocking chair outside, holding a cup of coffee and an inevitable cigarette in her long, old fingers. She would watch Michael's car approach with squinted eyes, as if measuring him up and down, and as he came out of the car and walked toward her, she would nod with approval and jump to her feet almost too quickly for her age. She always said the same thing: "Hi Doc, I think this time I have something really special for you." And she surely did. Michael never left without a treasure.

The dark corner in the back of the warehouse was one of his favorite places. Customers wouldn't go there and they weren't really expected to, for this place was home to hundreds of antique photographs collected from different sources over the years. Material possessions went fast, but yesterday's faces weren't in demand. Out of respect Clarice stocked them in a box in the corner. Michael loved that corner. He would pick up an old album and leaf through its fragile pages, looking at every face with complete attention as if hoping to find a familiar face among the strangers. He hadn't yet seen any familiar face in a conventional way — no relatives, no look-a likes, but every time he found a photograph or two of faces that looked dear to him. The old photographs possessed the magic of time. It felt precious to know that these people had lived their lives but were long gone, and along with them their dreams, secrets, their pain, their deepest fears. Michael felt close to them, it was as if he were able to connect with them directly through his heart, with no filters. So many of the faces were full of self-awareness, and that feeling of connection was incomparable to any of Michael's real life encounters. It touched him so deeply, he almost felt like crying a few times. In these moments he became acutely aware of how fragile, yet how connected and interdependent humans were, as if they all were one organism evolving through time through the fates of separate people.

He loved antique statues and sculptures, too. Clarice knew it, and by some magic was able to find Michael his most treasured possessions. One of Michael's favorites was a wooden statue of Buddha that Clarice had found somewhere in the Southwest desert. Nobody knew how old it was and refinishing took a bit of work — Michael had to clean it, polish and color it, and finally massage it with teak oil. The Buddha seemed content and happy as it stood shining in Michael's bedroom. It wasn't a religious symbol for Michael. He didn't identify with any religion. He grew up in a Midwest Catholic family, but most of his childhood religious conditioning was left behind by his exploration of the human mind. For him, religion was a fairytale and as much as Michael wanted to believe in fairytales, he was a grown man with a developed rational mind. Such a mind couldn't compromise to any religious dogma. The Buddha's intrinsic value was based only on the beauty of its form, and nothing more.

The garden was home to his two most precious statues. They were placed on each side of the arch, marking the entrance to the deepest part of the garden and its dark, tall trees and hills. The figures were a life-sized male and female reflecting each other symmetrically. They were twins and hunters. The woman held a bow in her left hand and an arrow in her right hand, pressing it against her right breast, tip down. Her left breast, perfect in its form, was exposed while the rest of her figure was covered with a flowing tunic. A quiver of arrows was slung across her back. The man had a belt fastened around his chest, the same set of arrows behind his back, and an obedient dog at his feet watching his master's face with utmost loyalty. The intricacy of detail in their faces, clothes, and hunting gear was such that Michael knew he'd purchased something special. It was his best investment ever: Clarice had charged him only three thousand for both.

"I have no idea where they came from," Clarice had told him. "An old man had purchased them for his estate long ago, but since his wife died he's practically been giving all his treasures away, God bless his soul." Clarice had squinted her eyes with pleasure when she told this to Michael. She had obviously made quite a deal on the end of that estate. Michael didn't need to know more. "Twin Gods" she put on the invoice. He loved these figures greeting him in the morning and after a while they became a family to him. He grew to care about them as if they were real beings.

Today he felt that the woman's gaze was fixed on him with particular intensity — he always had a much stronger connection with her than with her twin. An old yellow stain on her forehead deposited there by time was lit by emerging sunrays and made her eyes more alive than ever. It was almost as if she were trying to tell him something.

Suddenly a large crow flew down and landed on a nearby tree branch. It was intensely black and shiny as if someone had just washed it with shampoo. The bird jumped down the branch, strongly and confidently, turning its small head briskly from right to left while training its black shiny eye on Michael. The crow cawed a few times in a deep, raspy voice. Michael couldn't tell whether it was a scream of pleasure or distress; it could have been easily both. And then it flew off as suddenly as it had appeared. The Goddess' stone eyes were still fixed on Michael and the whole scene became so intense and magical that Michael had to shake his head and remind himself to hurry up not to be late to work.

As he entered the hospital building, he tried to walk confidently through his ward to cover the pain from the bruise, but he felt with his skin how his patients evaluated his every step, the same way they'd been doing for years. Most had learned to recognize Michael's mood before he even spoke a word, determining it through the physical pattern of his entrance when his key turned in the keyhole and the door shot wide open and he marched like a monarch to meet his awaiting subjects. They would be patiently waiting, hoping that today might be the day they get to spend more time with him, get a piece of his considerate attention, his compassion and sometimes profound insight.

But today was different. Somebody who didn't obey Michael's rules lived inside his kingdom. Somebody who, even when locked up behind the maximum-security gates, still managed to have more freedom than most people enjoy in their lives outside. Or did he? Maybe it was only the hypnotic power of the man's psychopathic mind that was finally catching up with Michael's own, causing him to experience rare moments of doubt. Michael liked this idea; it made him look temporarily weak. But only temporarily. Ultimately, he would regain all the control. It would be a great learning experience.

Michael's first patient was Rogers — a schizophrenic for more than thirty years, disheveled, confused, with occasional moments of lucidity. Michael's professional goal for Rogers was to ensure his physical comfort and well-being, nothing more than that; the disease seemed to have taken away anything beyond that.

"What is your goal in life, Mr. Rogers? Do you have any?" he asked almost mechanically, without expecting a sensible answer.

The patient's eyes focused for a moment as if his mental chatter had suddenly stopped. It was a clear moment when he looked directly at Michael and said, "To grow wings and fly away."

Michael smiled as if listening to a child sharing a beautiful naïve fantasy. "It's a nice goal, I suppose."

"I am getting there." Rogers' speech became more intense. "You see, I feel like my spine expands and all the muscles in my back are getting so strong and they start pulling so even the bones crack sometimes, I can hear it..."

Michael had no intention of following this tangent. "Tell me about your parents a little, Mr. Rogers, are they still around?"

The man stopped abruptly, furrowed his brow, then suddenly assumed an air of superiority that only psychotic people can exhibit, superiority that knows no bounds and only complete determination.

"Don't patronize me, you moron! You are a part of their conspiracy too, aren't you?! Then you should know that I don't believe in such things as Mom and Dad. I was brought up by a special force." His eyes were cold and detached, little balls of steel rooted deeply on a gray, wrinkled, amorphous face.

There was no point in continuing. The case was clear and straightforward. Michael's mood changed dramatically though. It shifted from compassion and care toward tension and anger. He observed it carefully, and decided that the anger was targeted at mental illness itself, illness that turns people's minds into such a helpless existence void of any meaning. He had witnessed it for so many years, unable to change the destructive course of this evil force that had no mercy on the people it possessed.

Michael also noticed a slight sense of relief behind his anger. He recognized this relief. It came from the fact that he was spared, that his mind was safe and protected and he would never go through disintegration like this. He accepted the fact that he was scared to death of losing his mind and becoming like one of his patients, and had determined long ago he would do anything to protect his sanity.

He closed the chart and put it away. "You can go to your room, Mr. Rogers," Michael said calmly, his voice surrounding the enraged patient like a soothing envelope.

The patient's face relaxed, his fighting stance eased, he silently nodded, acknowledging that he would go to his room voluntarily. Before leaving Michael's office, though, Rogers turned back, looked directly at Michael. The vicious fire of insanity still burned deep inside his eyes as he spoke, laughing wickedly. "It's funny how you can't see it behind your own sheep's skin, you are the same predator as he.... Funny you can't see it though." He slammed the door behind him as he exited.

Michael didn't need to ask. He knew Rogers was talking about Theodorus. It seemed that his new patient was able to penetrate the unconscious minds of many, including even the most impaired schizophrenics.

Michael took a deep breath and resolved that he would focus only on the interest this man evoked in him and not let his emotions be part of today's conversation with Theodorus. He felt calm again and only then he called the staff to bring Theodorus in.

"Let's talk about your charges today, Mr. Theodorus. As a general rule, I don't go into these discussions with my patients. After all I am a psychiatrist, not a lawyer. But in your case, I think your understanding of the charges that are being brought against you can help me understand what is going on in your mind. Even though, as always, you don't have to talk to me about it if you don't feel like it."

"I feel like it."

Michael looked down and noticed that Theodorus had brought a folder with him. He placed it carefully on the edge of Michael's desk and opened it slowly as if it contained a fragile treasure. He looked tired and even thinner today. *His sleep is probably insufficient*, Michael thought.

"This is what she wrote in the solitude of her apartment," Theodorus said contemplatively as he browsed through loose pages covered with neat small handwriting.

"Green lamp lit over her desk, her hair down her shoulders, hand moving over the paper quickly.... Don't ask me how I know the details — I might say I have imagined it all, or I might say that I had been stalking her for a long time and came to learn the slightest details of her routine. Both things can be true and both can be lies. Don't waste your energy trying to figure it out.

"I know that she wrote those letters in solitude, in a state that I can only call a psychic fever — a fever that attacked her mind, her emotions, and more than anything, her soul and her soul's hope. What you see before you now are her letters, well, replicas of them.

I did not make the slightest change when I copied them by hand, one by one. I had to destroy the originals for obvious reasons. The letters were the only things I took from her. I left everything else untouched. Do you realize that her body was never found? That's why we are here talking, because the DA has only circumstantial evidence against me and they are buying time by sending me here 'to restore my competency.' Anyway, here it is. Go ahead, take the folder. Read the letters. But I have to warn you, they gave me chills when I was copying them."

Michael gave Theodorus a long look. He realized that this conversation was useless as forensic evidence — he didn't confess to murder and he could have made it all up, out of boredom or out of his never-ending desire to play mind games. This one was a good game though, Michael had to admit, and the next logical step in sustaining the game was to read the letters. Theodorus had put a lot of effort in preparing this material. Michael took the folder and let Theodorus go. He pushed the folder aside on his desk, thinking to come back to it tomorrow. But then he couldn't let it go. The folder kept calling to him. *Like a siren*, he mused, allowing himself a knowing smile. He pulled the folder close and opened it. The letters were folded in order from the earliest dates to more recent. The handwriting was neat and easy to read and then Michael remembered that it was actually Theodorus' handwriting. The letters were addressed to the same person but nowhere did she (if they really were her letters) mention his name. None of them were signed. Michael opened the first one carefully.

9.

October 12

Have you ever thought that love is a disease, a sickness so powerful, like a virus, that you can't even see when and how it enters you? You can only have a premonition, a guess at best, yet it is already in you, making its morbid accommodations inside your soul but you don't have any symptoms yet, you are still oblivious to this unstoppable force that is about to change your life forever. That is what happened to me when I met you. At first there was just a slight vibration in the air when somebody pronounced your name as one of the guests for our conference. The vibration remained for a little while. I noticed it, but didn't make anything out of it. Still, looking back I can see clearly that the gateway for the disease was prepared when I first heard your name. And when I was walking toward the arrival section at the airport to meet you along with the other guests and to accompany you to the hotel, my body was marching toward its destiny as if it already knew it and the floodgate opened the moment I looked into your eyes for the first time and saw myself in them and you shook my hand and smiled. You were so friendly and charming and confident with an air of kindness that I have not seen before and have never met after. Kindness was your trademark. That is what I miss the most in the world since you left.

Yet I will not give up this sickness for any price in the world. I never knew that just looking at the same things with another person and realizing that you see it together can give you such pleasure. I felt it when we were on the bus and you were sitting in the back and I had to turn to look at you because I knew exactly what you were feeling looking through the window. Then you looked at me and smiled as if you knew what was happening inside of me. My city, so known to me and so foreign for you, looked like a place I'd never seen before because our perceptions mixed and I just knew that you were me and I was you and we saw the rain and the small wooden houses soaked under it and a lonely wet dog running by the road through the same eyes....

So these are love letters? Michael scratched his left temple, contemplating what to do next. He had hoped the letters would give him clues to the crime. Michael felt irritated. *Fucking Theodorus! Another game just to keep me on my toes!* Yet the papers covered with neat handwriting continued to call to him. They were an intricate net luring him deeper into this woman's soul, inviting him to feel her pain and her ecstasy and more than anything to find out how her story had ended. He smelled tragedy at the end. Of course, she was presumed dead after all, it would be hard to picture a happy ending. Yet against his professional judgment, his knowledge of past events, some similar, some dissimilar, every fiber of his emotional being hoped for a miracle. Michael rarely felt consumed with such compassion. He witnessed tragedies on a daily basis; they became routine. It wasn't that he'd become numb to human suffering, but rather had learned how to be professionally detached so he could stay functional and provide help.

This woman affected him differently. Her voice, speaking from far away — *from where,* he wondered — made his heart ache in a manner Michael couldn't remember experiencing. He felt connected and associated with her, as if her story was his own even though he personally didn't remember experiencing a love like that. Finally, after a moment of internal debate, he gave in and kept reading despite other pressing matters.

November 17

It is my birthday today. And we never had a chance to celebrate it together. Not once. Sometimes I wonder how our life together would be if we had a chance to experience it more. And sometimes I feel like a greedy old lady who retains all the treasures that she collected over the years but still she is burning with desire for more and more and more! For her it is never enough. But my treasures are not possessions of this world, they are my memories of you and our time together, and yes, they are all safely locked in my golden box and God forbid anybody ever tries to take it away from me! But it's not enough. Even my dreams, my generous, magical dreams, that deliver me to you with such an ease and let me stay with you and live our second life somewhere behind the screen of a waking reality, they are finite, too. Morning sun forces me to open my eyelids, sounds of this world tear my consciousness away from you, the fog of forgetting rises between us and here we are again, separated by an omnipotent bridge nobody can cross.

Now, back to my birthday. I picture how it could have been — I know you would bring me flowers — tons of them, colorful, fragrant — and my favorite chocolate, and then you would sing something in your deep, loud voice, sometimes out of tune and I would laugh and you would get shy but then you would start laughing with me too. And then we would go dancing.

Sometimes I wonder if I should have separate boxes for my memories, one for the memories of things that really happened and the other for things I dreamed of or imagined? But you know what, the more time passes the less possible it becomes for me to separate them. The pictures, moves, and sounds mix; they penetrate each other, they float under my closed eyelids as one stream, causing the same sweet resonance in my physical beating heart. My memories and dreams of you are like my children and none of them is more loved than the other. Crazy, huh?

I know you would understand this. Remember your birthday that we did celebrate together? I ran all over the city arranging a cake for you, this white, fluffy, too sweet, ridiculous brick with glossy red 4 and 0 scrambled on top of it. And those four stupid little yellow candles. I really, really wanted you to like this cake. I knew it was pathetic and ridiculous and I was almost crying from disappointment when I brought it home. Yet when you saw it and smiled I knew you liked it. You were just like a happy kid, and then the 0 on the cake got smashed somehow when we put it on the table and you truly became a four-year-old kid in a candy store. But behind the childish joy and the messy cake with frosting everywhere, I caught a moment of you looking at me directly, no boundaries between us, as always, and you saw everything — how I wanted to please you and my anxiety that I was failing. You saw my mind going a million different directions until your eyes stopped me and then there was a moment of silence when everything else stood still and I knew how much you loved me.

I have another memory of your birthday, from just a few months ago. I didn't do anything that day, came home from work, tired. I did more translations in that day than in the whole month, probably to exhaust myself and forget that it was August 17. My little room was cold and dark, I didn't make dinner and I don't think I even remembered it was your birthday when I fell asleep, right on my couch, before I even changed my clothes.

The dream hit me right away, with almost no transition. I found myself in the same apartment, sitting on a little white kitchen chair by the balcony, window slightly open, so the smoke of my cigarette could escape. I was facing the window, it was dark outside, a heavy night with no stars. There was only a small, green table lamp lit next to my bed. I didn't hear you coming and I only realized that you were there when I felt your hand on my shoulder.

"Why are you crying, Piccolo?" I knew it was you before I heard your voice. I could never confuse your presence with anyone else's, even when I really wanted to and tried to. I didn't realize I was crying until you asked. Then I felt a cold layer of tears covering my face. I probably had been sitting by the window, crying, for hours.

"Because it is your birthday today and I can't even give you a gift."

"Sure you can...." I still didn't look at you, not because I was avoiding something but because I always perceived you in some perfect holographic way, all I needed was just one little piece of you, the sound of your voice, or a corner of your mouth, your laugh, a shadow of you walking away, any small fragment would be enough for me to bring you back instantaneously, your whole being in flesh and blood, with your humor and your personality. I always could feel your wholeness from the smallest memories of you.

"You are dead now, how can I possibly give you any gifts?" I answered.

"So?" you laughed gently, "you still can give me a gift if you want to."

"Like what?" I didn't want to sound resentful so as not to hurt your feelings, yet I realized I did.

"Well, let me think, I don't really need much.... Here is a good one. How about you stop smoking as a gift for me?"

I looked at you and saw your genuine smile and I knew you really meant it. With the sharpness of your mind, you had been brilliantly sarcastic with so many people in the past, but never with me.

"Why would it be a gift for you? You didn't die from lung cancer, you died in the accident."

"Well, first, you don't know that for sure, things are not always what they appear to be. And second, it would make me feel very happy if you stop putting this ugly, smelly, dirty stick in your mouth." And then you laughed again.

I looked at the cigarette butt, yellow-grey under the dim light with a trace of smoke coming out of it and I couldn't help but laugh myself. I pressed it into the ashtray, it crinkled under my fingers as if trying to save itself and then fell flat and I felt so happy and relieved. I stopped crying, I turned around and said "Happy Birthday!" You were right there, next to me, so real and alive, and you smiled and said "Thank you."

I woke up the next moment. My clock had stopped. I don't know how long I was asleep on the couch. I walked straight to the balcony, found an ashtray with yesterday's cigarette butt still in it, took it to the kitchen, threw it in the garbage, cleaned the ashtray and I haven't smoked since. Last year I had been smoking a pack a day, easily, I heard so many lectures from my friends, how I was not taking care of myself, how I was damaging my health and frankly it was tiring to smoke that much. I had tried to stop then, yet the craving, the withdrawal was not worth the efforts and I kept smoking.

But after that dream, every moment when I felt the urge to smoke I felt an unbelievable joy; feeling the urge and choosing not to smoke was like giving you a birthday gift again and again. I almost felt disappointed when the cravings went away.

So now you have it, two birthday memories — one dream, one real. What is more real and what is less? I cherish and remember them both. They are equally real for me. Do you think I am going crazy?

No? You just wanted to wish me a Happy Birthday, is that what you would say? Sometimes I swear I hear you so clearly. Why can't I completely believe that you are still near me? Why?

Michael had to stop reading. Her words were hypnotic and poignant; they made him more emotional than he could allow himself to be, at least within the hospital walls. He tried to remind himself that it was Theodorus' handwriting and that there was no proof this wasn't anything more than one of his clever tricks. But he couldn't buy that. The woman's voice was unquestionably genuine and distinct. There was no way Theodorus could have made up this kind of writing. Michael pushed the letter aside. He found her style and her obsession somewhat annoying, yet he did feel sorry for her, it was hard not to. *She must have lost her father early in life*, he thought to himself, yet it didn't explain everything in her character. She remained enigmatic and evasive, as if she were challenging him through her writing without ever meeting him.

She wrote as if she were still making love to her lover. At that thought, Michael shivered. He had felt it too. As if someone from far away were making love to him.

"This is insane," he said aloud. The sound of his own voice surprised him. There was a crack in it, a fragility he found both unfamiliar and frightening.

He shook his head, trying to shake the moment away. He forced his attention to the facts.

She had been missing over six months. The only possible key to finding her remains and putting closure to her story belonged to a madman who was locked up in this hospital. Yet he was playing games and showing no signs that he would cooperate any time soon. Michael pushed the letter farther away, to the edge of his desk, consciously restraining himself from allowing another personal reaction.

Just another human tragedy. He witnessed it every day. There was nothing in this story that needed his healing, the tragedy had played out the way it did, no changes were possible. Why couldn't he forget about it and get back to work?

Michael didn't know the answer, but if he had paid attention to what was really bothering him he would have been surprised to realize that deep down he was hoping for one thing and one thing only, and that he was willing to do whatever it took for that thing to happen. Yet he didn't allow himself to ponder, and it remained hidden from him that what he wanted more than anything was for these two people he never met to find each other again.

Because when they did, everything would change for him, too.

10.

Michael left his desk, walked to the unit, got a report from his staff, talked to some patients, chatted with night shift staff who were about to go home after a long, stressful night. He was his usual self, warm, attentive, present, and in control. No one he talked to that morning noticed anything different about Michael, or so he thought. Yet his mind was fighting the force of those letters, he couldn't forget them for a moment. The invisible mental magnet hidden inside those loose white papers spread out on his desk pulled him back to keep reading.

That afternoon, he stopped fighting and went back to his office, locked the door, turned off his phone and read the rest of the letters. He carefully folded them, put them inside his desk drawer, put on his long, black wool coat, locked his office door and walked away. He walked through the halls without looking at people, hoping that no one would notice him or the traces of tears on his face. It wasn't until he'd left the unit that he thought he'd seen Theodorus watching him from the shadows. He didn't want to know what the psychopath had seen.

Most patients were attending therapy groups and the halls were nearly empty, but Michael pressed forward as if fighting through a crowd. For the first time he became afraid that one of his episodes would happen inside the security walls. Never before had Michael even allowed himself to consider that an option. He knew that he didn't really have any control of his episodes, yet he had always felt certain that they wouldn't happen in public, especially in the hospital. He likened this to "la belle indifference" experienced by a young, histrionic paraplegic female patient Michael used to consult. The woman couldn't walk because of a deep unconscious, psychological conflict, yet she would present herself happy, smiling and not the least bit concerned about her paralysis. Deep down in her unconsciousness, she knew her condition wasn't permanent and could be resolved at any time. Now that his denial was cracking under the pressure, Michael's defenses were thinning, evaporating, leaving him vulnerable and exposed to his own investigating mind. His growing internal panic led him to escape the hospital in order to preserve his evading safety.

He walked with his head down and eyes lowered. His walk was rhythmic and paced and as much as he tried to push them away, the letters kept echoing in his mind against his will. He had read each of the letters twice and they wouldn't let him go. His reality became fluid and the words from the letter drummed in his head, connected to the rhythm of his steps; they jumped around him, bounced off the walls as if making those very walls flexible and illusory. In Michael's mind he could clearly see this woman sitting on the train, in a small, yet comfortable compartment, looking outside the window, watching the vast and calm nature outside blur by, adjusting her pen to the lurch and jerk of the train as she wrote.

The letters had etched into his mind. The certainty of their perfect presence both excited and frightened him. He had always had a good memory, but this was different. He knew every word.

> I woke up this morning so happy. I don't know if it was the train moving, or my resolution to finally allow myself to believe, or you trying to comfort me from out there. Whatever brought me this dream last night, I can't thank it enough. In that dream, I spent my whole night with you, in a small beachside town, something beautiful, warm and unique, like Santa Barbara. We

stayed in a local hotel. We walked around, ate in a little family-owned restaurant, did some shopping in a beachside boutique, went back to our hotel room, made love in the afternoon and then went dancing at night. Every moment of that dream was real, alive, and so deeply emotional. I could sense again what it felt like to be so happily in love. You were you, complete and unmistakable you, my beloved. We were in the beginning stages of our dating, with some things still awkward and uncertain. You asked me if I could come and stay with you in your family home next, and I got panicked. I always felt intimidated by the old aristocratic background that you came from and that I knew so little about. "I don't know, I feel kind of scared," I answered. "What if I do things wrong and make mistakes and your family will not accept me?"

You laughed and looked at me with such kindness again and then you said, "Remember, I have died already. Don't you think we can feel easy about rules and ceremonies like this by now?" And it felt so normal and reassuring somehow. Right before we parted in the morning after checking out of the hotel, you paused with hesitation and asked me in a soft voice, "So you do want to see me again?" "Of course," I said, "why do you even ask?" "Because I want to make sure that you like being with me, that you like making love to me." I looked at you and laughed, realizing suddenly that you were the one who felt insecure and needed reassurance. "Please don't tell me you have performance anxiety now, or do you?" "Well, I just want to make sure that you like making love to me."

"But I thought you said you had died already so we can let all the fears go, right?" "Yeah... but some things die hard, Piccolo." We both burst into laughter, knowing as deep as deep goes that there is nothing more

beautiful, safe, and transforming than us making love
to each other.

Michael felt the air thin as he approached the security gate. The
feeling from that letter enveloped him like a cloud, he had breathed
it in and the feeling penetrated him, changing something inside. He
tried to focus on simple tasks of returning his keys, scanning his ID,
saying good night to the evening staff, but as he was about to enter
the door to leave, a large, black crow flew above his head, circled over
him, made a loud gargling sound and flew through the door ahead of
Michael.

Michael's heart froze, his veins tensed, and his neck muscles got
so stiff that he couldn't look around to see other people's reaction to
the strange event. It was impossible. Not even a small bug could get in
through thick, concrete walls and sealed, bullet-proof windows, and
yet the crow had been inside. People walking in and out greeted each
other as if nothing odd had happened. Michael wondered if he had
imagined the whole thing.

Michael almost ran to his car, a small, black Mercedes, parked in a
designated spot — he had been with the hospital long enough to earn
the privilege of an assigned parking space. The car started right away
and Michael drove away as fast as he could, to the obvious surprise
of the hospital police officers patrolling the grounds. They let Michael
go without chase.

He took a highway and without thinking he drove away from the
familiar landmarks, east, to a remote state park. Forty miles down the
road he was in a wild forest. He didn't remember having ever come
here before, yet somehow it all seemed familiar. He parked at the end
of a paved road, took off and started walking into the woods, his long
coat brushing off small bushes, his head up, looking at the treetops,
his mind in flames. He started to run just to burn away the frustration
and confusion, but three steps into the run he began to feel more
relaxed. He slowed again to a walk and started to feel comfortable
again.

As he wandered the forest, Michael remembered a late summer
afternoon in his childhood right after his parents divorced. He had felt
so out of place, so un-needed and unnoticed by family members who

were fighting bitterly over the divorce. An only child, Michael didn't have anyone to share his pain with, and at fifteen his identity had already been shaped anyway — he did not show emotion. Showing emotion was a sign of weakness, so said and lived his father, who was becoming frighteningly estranged each day he lived apart from Michael and his mom.

On that summer afternoon, he had walked for a long time, far from home. He walked to physically soothe the feeling of being lost. He walked in a straight line, hoping such determination might give him the sense of direction he was missing. He walked for hours until he wandered into the forest. Suddenly, the reality outside of the modern city came over him like a wave, silencing all anxiety, making all his fears irrelevant.

Michael walked deeper into the forest and the childhood memory became more alive with every step. Little Mike was walking in the forest beside him, within him, tears on his face, that sinking feeling in his stomach. He was a scared child trying to run away from a disaster that had torn his world apart, and a grown man trying to walk away from a disaster that prepared to strike.

The sun was going down. It got cold and dark, yet the forest looked more and more familiar and strangely safe. He couldn't avoid analyzing the circumstance. Perhaps something was different in Michael's mind — maybe the concrete, solid wall that separated the different worlds he lived in wasn't absolute anymore. Perhaps some transparency was emerging, removing his denial, just a little, yet enough for his resistance to weaken. He walked farther into the forest, knowing that an episode was coming over him. For the first time he welcomed it without fear. As he began to transform, the rest of the letters flashed through his mind again and he felt profoundly grateful to this woman who had evoked changes in him deeper than he could ever hope for.

March 12

This is my final letter to you. I feel that it is, and my feelings haven't lied to me lately.

I am taking the train again, returning home from a short vacation. The train is moving forward with comfortable pushes, my tea is still hot in a glass teacup that the carriage attendant provided and it reflects the sun outside as a small flicker jumps around my cabin. The sound of the train wheels is rhythmic and predictable and it makes this journey comfortable, safe. The sense of moving externally and internally is so balanced now that I feel at complete peace and acceptance with my decisions. I have grown a lot. I wish you could see me now, the person I have become because of you and because of my love for you. I think you would like me in this new state. That's why, I guess, I changed this way, transforming myself toward the ideal woman that I anticipate you might fall in love with. I have become that woman, once again, after I lost myself for a while having lost you.

I know it's been a while since I wrote you last. But something in me knows that I am writing more for myself than for you, not because you will never be able to read this but because now I know as deep as deep goes that you are here and you know what is happening to me and you can see inside my heart. You know by now that I moved away, that I finalized my divorce (I don't think he even noticed), that I found a great job (thank God for English!) and how much I enjoy decorating my cute, little beachside apartment. You also know by now that I have tried to move on and to have relationships with other people. "Tried" is the key word. I guess when you have to try to have a relationship it is obvious that love is not there. I had never had to try anything with you. I didn't even have to try to survive your death. I went through it as if it were a heavy, inflamed, liquid metal sticking to my skin, blocking my every move, burning my lungs with every breath I took with never ending pain. But I didn't try to end it or survive it; all I did was look to find a way to be with you again. And I think I finally did.

I am not suicidal; if killing myself were the way to go to you, I would have done it long ago. But I know that it's not. I love life, I love being alive, waking up in the morning and realizing that my consciousness is back in this world with all its beauty, and its chaos, and fascination. I love walking out on my steps and seeing the morning sun, and hearing a little bird chirping on a small, green bush, and kids laughing and running somewhere in the background. I love this world more and more with each passing day and it fascinates me to notice every time when something brings a memory of you — a sound, or somebody's shadow on the road, the open sky we used to look at together — that as much as I love this incredible world, I love you even more.

Isn't it amazing how one person can become equivalent to the immense totality of everything else on this planet? Sometimes I look at myself feeling this love and feel in awe and sometimes I ask myself why this man is so dear to me, why do I feel such a love? I don't know. But I do know now that there is a way for me to find you and not lose anything in this world. I am going to take this path. When you were looking at me, I always felt as if your eyes had a powerful, yet invisible magnet in them. A magnet that was able to gather together all different pieces of me, even remote parts of myself that I didn't yet know or remember. Under your gaze all parts of me danced together into one complete pattern, which was my soul looking at you, and it was beautiful and complete. And now for me to take this path, all I need to do is follow the pull of this magnet until I stand before you again and you can look at me and smile.

I've been in communication now for quite some time with a person I found on the Internet. I haven't met him yet, but I am going to tonight, right after the opera. Did I mention to you that I have a ticket to the new Master and Margarita opera? Isn't it amazing that they finally produced it on stage? Remember how we discussed it for hours and how we both loved this book so much even though it was for completely different reasons? Well, I am going to see it tonight and then if everything goes according to

plan I am going to meet this person and he is going to help me find you. The rest is history. I love you. And I always will.
    N.

11.

Michael, the wolf, looked around and saw no signs of life. The fading afternoon sun lit the hill. The forest on his right looked darker with each passing moment. His body started twitching all over. He had little time left here before the transformation took him back to his human world. Yet he knew he had to make it to the other side of the hill before it happened. Something was there, he could smell it.

He tensed his muscles and made a jump, as far as he could and then ran, first up the hill, breathing intensely as with each forced exhale he pushed his body higher. Soon he reached the top. He could still see the other side of the hill perfectly well. It wasn't as steep as the side he had just conquered; it looked almost like a peaceful valley, an open, large meadow, covered with clever flowers and tall grass that moved gently under the breeze. Everything looked familiar. Michael sensed the knowing of this place with a thirst for memories it evoked, warm, tender, innocent memories of home he had carried inside as a child. He almost choked from this feeling of knowing when he saw the house down the hill. A white, castle-like house. Simple, yet unique, strange, yet familiar.

He watched with keen lupine eyes as a door opened and a man stepped outside to look at the setting sun. Michael could tell he was a happy man by the way he opened the door and stood at the doorstep: relaxed, content, contemplating his surroundings, carrying no fears, no anxieties, dressed in a casual white shirt and dark pants. He stood barefoot at the door, watching the sunset. He was waiting for some-one. And that somebody was inevitable. Michael was sure the man knew it and had all the patience. Michael knew many things about this man — things he shouldn't have known simply from observation.

The man loved the sun at this hour; sometimes he would sit at the table in the garden, drinking tea, watching sunset at the horizon. He would always come out at this hour. He would always wait, day after day, one sunset after another.

Michael knew then that he would return as well — or had he been here already before? — to watch the man from under the bushes. He wanted to be there when that someone finally arrived. He needed to be there. He couldn't miss that moment for anything. On this day, the man didn't stay out long. He lifted his head, looked at the sky, twilight blue with a hint of darkness just starting to gather for the night. The man smiled a kind and genuine smile, then went back to the house, closing the door behind him gently.

Michael's body started twisting. He crouched under the dark bush; its sharp, needle-like leaves were pricking his skin, reaching un-der his long fur, but the pain couldn't stop the wave from coming. It pulsated its way into his brain. He felt like he was going up and down on a giant swing, wind blowing in his face with the force of a hurri-cane. His body rocked, moved, pushed through a gate, as if he were being born again, and then everything went blank. When he woke up in the safety of his home, the wall between two worlds was more solid than ever. His denial had sensed the cracks and reinforced itself, making sure that no memory from the magical life in the forest could enter Michael's human mind.

12.

Before Michael even sat down, Theodorus broached the subject of the letters in his trademark straightforward manner that Michael, despite his dislike for Theodorus, had begun to find appealing.

"They really make you think about the nature of love, those letters, don't they?" he said.

"Well, that and many other things," Michael answered. "What do you think about the nature of love, Mr. Theodorus?"

"Essentially it is a need for shape-shifting." His eyes were intent, steel drills focused on Michael's face. Michael sensed that not a single muscle twitch on his face would escape Theodorus' attention. He was okay with that. Michael had mastered a level of comfort with this patient that would be hard to disturb.

"What do you mean by that?"

"Think about it. Love is a force more powerful than anything known in human history. Power, money, lust, sex, pain, fear — they are all ultimately subservient to love. Love is the commander-in-chief of all human emotions, whether we allow ourselves to admit it or not. And the ultimate goal in any love experience is to merge with someone other than ourselves, to become one with someone outside of us. That woman was not an exception."

Michael noticed Theodorus used the past tense in his mention of the woman, but said nothing. He kept listening, sitting in his comfortable office chair, his body relaxed, but his mind super alert.

"Well," continued Theodorus, "I understand that my remark requires some background explanation since it is based on a completely different concept of reality."

"Different from what?"

"From the established consensus. In my worldview the statement that 'reality as we know it is an illusion' has a completely different implication than in other known systems. Consider Buddhism. They emphasize the transitory, unreal nature of our material universe, including our physical bodies and even our identities. And that's fine with me. The next step in their reasoning though I find quite outdated. The idea of 'detaching from this world' since it is merely an illusion may have been a reasonable suggestion in the time of Buddha when material existence for most people on the planet was painful and hardly bearable. But not so much in our times. Why on Earth would I detach from all the goods, comforts, pleasures, and technologies only because some sensitive dude a few centuries ago thought it was a good idea?

"I share the same belief that reality is illusory, holographic, multidimensional, but my postulate is the opposite — 'attach.' I don't mean grab as hard as you can to any single material possession that comes your way. No. By 'attach' I mean 'create.' Create your own universe by attaching to your experiences creatively, by playing with this reality, by shape-shifting, by being in love with it. Then everything is possible. Then everything truly is love. Think about this — when we are looking for a 'once in a lifetime love,' we are searching to experience our own state of mind elevated above constraints of what seems to be rigid material existence. Love can take us there. Love can elevate us high and teach us how to be whomever we want or feel like being. No limits, no judgment, no reservation. I believe she experienced a glimpse of that freedom in love with the man she lost and when she had lost him, nothing in life could measure up to the pleasure of freedom that that affair had given her. So she had to shape-shift and leave. Just like Margarita did in that story. Was she murdered? Did she kill herself? Did she annihilate her material body with the power of her passion?

I know you want the answer to that, and you know I have it, but you need to be ready to perceive it."

"Here we go again." Michael furrowed his brow, fully aware that Theodorus would read this action as suspicion, as frustration. "Please spare me."

"You think I'm playing games here, don't you? Your prejudice against me is what fixates your inability to see. Who am I to say something of importance to you? A charming manipulator, a sociopath, a criminal, a rapist, possibly a murderer, you know better than to trust anything I say. But why?"

Theodorus paused, but his gaze didn't relax even a little. He wiped his nose with his arm in a motion that Michael had first thought a nervous tic. Now he wasn't so sure. Theodorus resumed speaking before his arm returned to his side.

"Coming back to your question about love, I think it is happening to you because, as is the case with the majority of modern people, you are disconnected from your love life. That's why your mind in its routine experience can't shape-shift. I have no reason to confuse you, no reason to take you away from the truth; in fact, my goal is the opposite. I see it now, Mr. Gate. It's obvious in your eyes. Your instinct tells you that I am telling the truth. Yet, the conditioned part of your mind keeps holding this mirror of illusion before your eyes, whispering, 'You can't trust him.' Being in love is an instinct, one of the primary ones; when it is activated everything else functions at a higher level. A state of natural high, that's what love it. The state of natural high during which our ability to shape our reality and to create our destinies is at its highest. Oh, and you know this — it doesn't have to be romantic or sexual, even though romanticism and sexuality are part of all forms of love."

He wiped his nose with his sleeve again, despite any evidence of a cold or sniffles. *Always with the left arm,* thought Michael.

"Any more questions, Mr. Gate?"

Michael paused for a moment and asked himself the million-dollar question: What is love? Michael thought of the flashes, bits of memory, and touches of complex feelings that sometimes came over him like warm waves. Those flashes were often prompted by something simple and unpredictable — the background Sade song at a restaurant, a trace of perfume left by an unfamiliar woman who walked by and disappeared around the corner, the cruelty of a biting winter wind touching his face outdoors. Instances like these made him long, deeply, passionately, terribly to tear up the fabric of reality and put his face into the safety of her warm, overwhelming, welcoming substance. He felt her presence in those moments and hers was the only safe and familiar presence in this strange world. And yet still she remained unknown to him despite these moments of longing and searching.

He thought it wasn't love itself but the anticipation of it. He thought it was an innate human drive — to strive for love but never able to find it. The stories of romance in the state hospital never ended, some tragic, some ridiculous. The hospital grounds knew so many secrets. Was it love when every year the police would escort out two, three female staff members who had become emotionally involved with patients? Not just mental patients, but criminally insane ones. Was it love that made them break the ultimate boundaries and fall into such dangerous men? And what of all the crimes of passion that had brought so many to the hospital? Was that love? The storylines were different, but the passion was all the same.

Michael had come to believe he simply wasn't supposed to experience what other people called love and by this time he had let go of any anticipation of it. Michael had trained his mind not to follow the pattern of empty thinking, and this included mechanical ruminating about love. At some point in his personal development, he had determined that the best book he could ever read on any subject is the one he could write himself, write in his mind and in his body. He became the embodiment of his thinking and guarded his train of thoughts from mental garbage. He wanted his book to be clean, precise, and entertaining. That's why he avoided contemplating vague subjects. So when he asked himself, what is love exactly, it was quite a mental departure for him.

"Have you been in love, Mr. Theodorus?"

"Oh, many times." Theodorus laughed openly, obviously enjoying himself. "Possessed, obsessed, heartbroken, ecstatic, lost, confused, angry, you name it. Yet I haven't completed my experience with love and that is why I can't achieve the privilege of my death as I told you.

But there I go again, confusing you unnecessarily. To answer your question more concretely, I am alone now and I have nothing even remotely close to the love story that you have."

Michael looked at him in disbelief. No personal reference was allowed in conversation with patients and they all were well aware of it. Discussing personal information about staff was considered a "cold threat" and could result in restriction of privileges.

"Look, this is it. I am not playing your games. I am not going to 'get ready' to perceive your answer. Go back to your room, Mr. Theodorus. That is enough for today. When you are ready to talk, you know how to find me."

"You're the boss."

Theodorus stood, paused for a moment, looking straight at Michael, then said very quietly under his breath, "You are not who you think you are." Then he silently left the room, no trace of emotional reaction visible on his face.

Michael felt awful. Beyond feeling bad about the abrupt and incomplete interview, he sensed something inside that troubled him even more. The feeling was so unsettling that he was afraid to explore it or name it. Something was happening to him that hadn't happened for a long time.

Michael had begun to doubt himself. This made him afraid.

13.

Raphael had decided to keep it simple. The decision was made early in rehearsal and was never questioned.

Pure emotion over performance sophistication. That is how Raphael saw it. The intentional simplicity evoked intense emotions in the audience, most of whom were vaguely familiar with the strange plot from the past. Keeping it simple ensured that all oddities, cultural confusions, and strange characters were eliminated, allowing the story to speak a modern person's emotional language as directly and as profoundly as possible. "Love never dies" was the main message, regardless of culture or century.

The stage was decorated in a simple theatrical manner. Urban details were cosmopolitan and easy to understand for a person from any culture. The daily lives of the characters were simplified so it left them in their pure roles — a man and woman in love with each other. Period. The mystical, dark, nightly part of the story was contrasted by changes in color, lights, costumes, and the feelings provided by the anticipation and the music, but he used no magic tricks. All the miracles and horrors happened in the audience's psyche, the stage was just a simple reflection of it.

Raphael knew that people would happily follow structure when it was well-developed and maintained. In that way, there was no difference between constructing an opera and a supermarket for shopping. People would follow the allure if it promised to make them feel good, and Raphael had learned how to accomplish that successfully through years of work. Only this time, the subject he was selling was one he had fallen for himself — love and its dominance over everything else.

The actors were well trained in a traditional way, their singing, dancing, and acting abilities were superb, and it seemed almost a miracle how quickly the casting had come together. The main actors showed up for audition on the first day as if guided by the characters themselves from some invisible, magical reality where all characters wait to be manifested into life. Everything felt "right" with the way the opera unfolded. The auditions, rehearsals, promotion, finances fell perfectly into place and tonight Raphael was witnessing the final product of this journey. He couldn't have been more pleased.

The stage darkened, with dim, red light coming from the floor lamps spaced evenly next to the walls. The light trembled slightly, almost below the level of perception, and strange, magical shadows moved swiftly through the walls. Magic was the essence of the performance. The book was magical, even decades after the collapse of the Soviet Union, after its prophets and architects were long gone and forgotten. The obscure, prosecuted writer of the book who never truly tasted his fame during his life and who silently faded away, was more magical and influential than ever. The sold-out opera performance was an endorsement to his creative power.

The music faded gradually until only a vague, subtle drumbeat came from under the stage. Raphael closed his eyes. After so many rehearsals, he still didn't feel ready to look at what was about to come. He was glad the theater was dark so nobody could see his face. He kept his eyes closed.

The rhythm intensified, turned into loud drumming, coming from all the corners of the stage. Raphael kept his eyes closed as he imagined what the audience was seeing — this is how he envisioned it for the first time inside his head — the drumbeat, the shadows first and then the strange images arising from under the floor, from hidden spaces — naked ladies, men dressed in tuxedos — all criminals, murderers, rapists of the past, moving out of the darkness toward the center of the stage where Margarita was standing now, naked and glorious, lit by the floor projectors, presiding over the Ball of Satan as its Queen.

It wasn't a story about philosophy, religion, faith, or even about good and evil. It was only about one woman's sacrifice for love, a deal with the Devil to become a witch just to return to the one she loved and had lost.

The audience watched her standing there in the center, surrounded by all the creatures trying to get to her and their reaction was mixed at first. Inhibition, social norm, and aesthetic expectations rushed through people's minds, creating tension and discomfort, yet the drumbeat pushed it away. Each strong pulse of the drum chipped away at those defenses, relaxed their minds, dissolved their fears. Some audience members started to rock gently in their chairs, some closed their eyes as Raphael did, and all of them drifted collectively into a trance with the woman's naked figure offering her vulnerability as a sacrifice for love, for each and every one of them. The opera was becoming a gate to enter the space of love.

Raphael recalled his words he wrote for the opera's program, directed then to an invisible audience. "Close your eyes, let the music flow.... Let the images on stage do their dance and take you far, far away, where there is no judgment, where fear is comforted and souls rest.... Let your soul fly with others as if there were no separation, just love and peace.... Let it all happen in your mind, let yourself fly and be carried into the joy of love... safely."

The characters took the stage one by one dancing in front of Margarita. Her body was motionless — she accepted her duty without resistance, knowing that she should greet every guest at Satan's ball with equal grace. The guests craved her attention. They jumped to the center one after another, male and female, all masked, aching for Margarita's approval. Each dancer used their moment of her attention with absolute passion. Their costumes were different but the masks were similar, a simple clay face bearing slightly different expressions, a feature distortion here and there invisible to the audience but perceived unconsciously. Their bodies wriggled, circled, jumped as they searched out Margarita's approval.

At first Raphael had considered using more specific masks, maybe even some depicting historical figures. But when he saw the first of these masks, made by a young props artist trained in Comédie-Française, he felt compelled to use them. Magic happened when the dancer had put on that first colorless mask. Everyone had seen the transformation in the dancer's movement. She became something new, something beyond the dancer herself.

When all the dancers had donned their masks for the first full dress rehearsal, the scene was mesmerizing. Their movements were unforgettable. Some crawling, some running in short strikes, as wild animals hunting, some marching overfilled with power and pride, some almost grotesquely exaggerated, yet, true to the core and alive. All of them, murderers, rapists, thieves were united by one strong desire — to be forgiven by Margarita, for she was so filled with love that it gave her power to forgive any sin.

Raphael opened his eyes, and watched the scene with relief. It was working precisely as planned. The archetypical rhythmic ritual, different bodies connected as one entity, a ceremony in which female beauty and devotion was bringing forgiveness through compassion. The performance had manifested in a precise way and Raphael felt how the audience responded profoundly. The air was charged by electricity from the opera — electricity that recharged people's souls. After all, isn't that what art is all about?

14.

A ray of sun burst through the heavy dark blue velvet curtain as if an invisible hand pulled it off. The light shot straight into Michael's eyes and before he could look at the alarm clock he instantly knew that he was late. Very late.

It looked like it was nearly afternoon. It had been an exhausting night and even though he didn't remember much, Michael knew he needed extra sleep. So he didn't feel terribly bad. He got up and performed his morning routine without rushing, the only exception being to skip running his three-mile treadmill run. His body felt sore and time was pressing.

He stepped outside with a coffee mug. The sky was high, the clouds were few and they glowed with turquoise glitter. It was breathtakingly beautiful, yet something was definitely off. The color combination, the touch of wind, the unusual warmth at this still early hour, everything was suspiciously strange. The days when something felt off were the worst days to be late to work. It was almost a given that something bad would play out during a full moon. On such days patients sensed it and acted out, even though repeated studies tried to prove there was no statistical correlation between natural events and agitation in the psychiatric hospital. Those who worked on the ground knew better, so much so that administration had to mandate people to work on full moon days.

Michael took a sip of his coffee and began to hurry to his car when a loud noise attracted his attention. He turned around and saw a large jet-black crow sitting atop the head of his female sculpture. The bird shook its wings, making itself comfortable.

"What the fuck?" Michael felt instantly enraged. This statue was his precious companion, his best investment. To see a large, dirty bird sitting on the statue's head was beyond Michael's tolerance.

He walked toward the crow slowly, looking straight into its eyes, stretching his right hand out as if he were about to grasp the creature's neck. The crow sat there without moving, defying common sense and logic, looking provocatively straight into Michael's eyes.

At some moment in this staring contest, it looked as if the crow was about to say something to him. Michael shook his head in disbelief and when he looked up again, the staring contest had ended. The crow looked away, jumped a few times on the statue's head, and with a loud caw took off and flew into the garden where it disappeared. Something small and shiny fell on the ground next to the statue's feet. Michael picked it up and laughed. Crows were notorious for stealing shiny objects, gold especially, and this one had found — and lost — something rather impressive. It was a golden heart with three small diamonds attached to it on a tiny, delicate chain. It looked rather like a charm, and certainly was very special and most likely expensive. Michael slipped it in his pocket and hurried to his car. It was going to be an intense day. Michael could feel it.

The list of patients who requested to see him was short and there were no new admissions to his unit. Theodorus seemed to be the only one who truly needed his attention today. Michael thought about their previous conversation and how inappropriate Theodorus had been to make up a story about Michael's love life. It didn't take long for Theodorus to reference the conversation. Clean-shaven, well rested, he looked younger by the day.

"Thank you for not taking away my privileges, Mr. Gate."

"Well, this is not kindergarten, Mr. Theodorus, you know the rules and I expect you to follow them without exception."

"Understood." Theodorus appeared cooperative and comforting and he looked like he really wanted to share something with Michael.

"So what is on your mind today, Mr. Theodorus?"

"Without getting too metaphysical, have you ever looked objectively at people's judgment? You've spent years in the forensic system that is precise and supposedly fair, supposedly. But all it does is create the illusion that life can be classified, dissected, filed neatly into appropriate boxes, with clear 'right' and 'wrong' labels on them. The irony of it all is that if you make one step away, just one little step and distance yourself just a little, you will see that those files are stored in one bigger box with the label 'bullshit.'"

"Please, Mr. Theodorus, spare me the theory of moral relativity."

"Why? Why should I spare you from that? Just because you want to dismiss it so your denial stays unharmed? Sorry, I'm not as big a fan of denials as you and millions of modern people are."

Michael still felt at ease in the conversation. He'd done it many times before. Just recently, he had a long philosophical discussion with a pedophile who tried to prove the existence of a special love bond between a boy and a man, citing references from antiquity and beyond. Michael remained calm and understanding as he listened to his patient, realizing fully that all his beliefs were arising from the patient's own story of growing up in a mobile park foster home, his parents long dead, and his white trash uncle and aunt doing drugs around the clock, remembering him only to blame him and beat him up for everything bad in the world. So when at seven years old he was sheltered by an old pedophile who gave him a sense of security and belonging in exchange for blow jobs, his world view was fixed. When this patient, as a grown man, lured little boys into sex, he truly believed it was a form of love.

Michael easily could handle conversations like that. They offered little but historical context to better understand patient makeup. In that case, Michael had concluded that the patient was beyond rehabilitation, with extremely high risk to reoffend. He recommended that the man not be paroled back to the community, period. His report was signed, sealed, sent to court. The patient will remain locked up for life, end of philosophical discussion.

Theodorus sat now in the chair across from Michael's table, dressed in a grey hospital uniform, his long hair down his shoulders, small reading glasses almost on the tip of his nose. He looked at Michael from over them. He seemed calm and benign; there was no sarcasm or opposition in his manner. He looked almost companionate.

Michael looked at him directly and reminded himself that his objective was to excavate Theodorus' delusional beliefs and help him prepare for the legal procedures of his case. Since his philosophy was an essential component of his delusions, Michael was glad to see that Theodorus was in the mood to talk.

"Go on Mr. Theodorus, I promised I will try to listen with no bias... I will try." Michael smiled genuinely. With most patients, his smile was his ultimate weapon, capable to charm the most dangerous snakes. With most patients. But not Theodorus.

"It is impossible. It is impossible to listen without bias, Mr. Gate, unless you are listening to music or sounds of nature. But when you are listening to an actual language, bias is inevitable. Language was created to impose bias. Language and bias are twin siblings connected at their heart; they can't exist without each other. And judgment is their little crippled sister dragging along for ages — sad human conditioning. Acquisition of language by humans reminds me of giving a toy train to a little boy who becomes so psychotically fascinated and entertained by it that he forgets to grow up. So when he is a man, he knows nothing else — he just keeps crawling in circles, following the train around its path to nowhere. When a grown man doesn't even know how to change his underwear, it's not cute anymore. To believe that the verbal description of reality is the only way to experience it is like wearing the same underwear for years, it's not cute, it stinks; the way judgment of most people does. I mean, this is Psychology 101. As you are contemplating how far you will let my philosophical inquiry go, I will make a remark on the nature of the sacred. You won't mind a little side trip into the realm of religion, will you?"

Theodorus didn't wait for an answer.

"I firmly believe that the only things that are sacred are the ones that help to solidify memories. The individual sacred solidifies individual memories, the collective — collective. The rest is bullshit. Humans are clay with high potential for self-awareness. When I say this, people get all offended as if I called them spineless. They wrongly assume the clay I'm referring to is molded by someone else and they don't want to perceive themselves as weak and submissive. In actuality, what I am saying is that our capacity for self-awareness gives us a magic opportunity to mold ourselves into anything of our choosing. Kids have that ability, but as they grow up they come to believe that they are solid structures, un-moldable creatures, when in fact, they are the very same clay, clay that just happened to lose self-awareness and become inflexible under the pressure of external circumstances. Sad, isn't it, Mr. Gate?"

"It's a nice metaphor..."

"It is less a metaphor than you would like to believe."

Michael had to admit, the way Theodorus addressed the most abstract subjects was compelling — he made the journey to his version of truth intriguing and fascinating on a visceral level. His question about religion punched Michael in the stomach. It took a moment to catch his breath. His own response scared and surprised him. For many years, anything connected with religion — the Catholicism he was born into as well as any other spiritual exploration he had done — seemed for him resolved, understood, and classified neatly in his mind. He had evaluated different meditations by the degree of their efficiency to produce relaxation. He collected spiritual writing from different traditions and revered his books as his cultural heritage, but no more than that. The image of God as a long-bearded old man keeping score in the sky had passed out and died right at a George Carlton concert. And that was fine with Michael.

However, today's conversation touched on something beyond Michael's religious inclinations. It aimed at the very center of his identity, and for the first time in his practice, he wanted to back off because he wasn't ready for that conversation.

"To answer your question about the semantics of religion would be a fascinating trip, Mr. Theodorus, I am sure. Maybe some other time. I would like to hear something more personal about you today. You haven't shared much of that yet. "

"Well, I guess I can combine the two by telling you a story. It happened one summer afternoon, in Chicago. I was walking through the parking lot of a small, suburban mall. The weather was nice, my business was going well, and I was settling into a relationship. I was getting my life together, so to speak.

"Don't expect any dramatic scene to follow, though. There was none. Yet something happened that afternoon that changed the course of my life. Something happened that moved it far from being 'together,' and into the realm of the unknown. I was passing a local coffee shop. People were sitting outside enjoying the sunny afternoon and as I walked by one of the fellows at the table on the corner cheered me with his beer and said, 'God bless you, man.'

"That was it. There were three of them sitting at the table, middle-aged black guys drinking their beers in the summer afternoon in Chicago. One of them just wanted to share their joy. And he really meant it, that guy, and it really hit me, like a blessing. But there was something else in the quality of his cheer that turned my life around, yet again. He saw me, and he was aware of communicating to me this wish and his support and his good intention and this awareness made all the difference. He knew how to deliver.

"I know it's hard to follow even though you're usually very good at catching nuances, but you don't get it yet, I can see that."

"I'm not sure I do," Michael admitted. "But it sounds like a moment of existential clarity."

"Yes! That's it!" Theodorus exclaimed. "You got it! The existential clarity, that was it. The interaction was a key and when it entered my mind it matched the lock and a gate was opened inside my mind that I didn't even know existed. It was an immediate understanding that our reality is limited, but not because we are afraid of the unknown, or because we are conditioned to limit our perception. All that may be true, but it is irrelevant. You see, the key to a limited perception of reality is the mechanism of how we create the experience of reality — through communication and through communication only. There is no other way around it. We stop communicating, our world stops, literally. There is no 'world' as we know it without us communicating it. We keep it going by constantly communicating, be it people, TV, fragments of our memories, our pets, letters we get, our computers — we do it all the time, so our worlds are uninterrupted. You see how simple it is? It's practically ingenious."

Theodorus looked as if he was going to wipe his nose with his sleeve again, but he appeared to stop the action before completing it. There was the beginning of a sly smile on his lips. He continued.

"Did you notice your reaction when I said this? Your mind jumped back to your ideas about my supposed grandiosity and all other options for your perception shut down. The pathway has been set."

Theodorus was right again, Michael had made that judgment; so he let it go for a moment and kept listening.

"Our capacity for communication is limited, we have to make a choice of what to pay attention to, and this is how we create the reality of our existence. Sometimes our focus is commanded so strongly by the forces outside of us that it becomes the only reality we know. Think about the guys here who hear voices. Regardless what the nature of those voices is, they are powerful enough to become the only communication channel in their minds and their minds get diseased and their realities collapse."

This time Theodorus completed the nose-wiping swipe of his arm.

"It doesn't mean you have to be afraid of it though," he said as he settled back into his chair.

The statement shook Michael. It was unsettling how this man seemed to know his innermost thoughts.

"Well, I just know it," said Mr. Theodorus. "But you are absolutely right. When you get these mechanics it is a moment of existential clarity. Nothing obvious happened to me as I smiled back to that man and kept walking in the sunny Chicago afternoon. But my life direction shifted, for I realized so clearly that for me to 'settle down and get my life together' would be equal to shutting down all other communication channels in my life and forgetting that I really can create my experience. I didn't want to do that. I wanted to expand my reality and I now had the key to do that — given generously by a man in a coffee shop. It was from him that I also learned that when we are aware of how life boundaries are being created it is our responsibility to help other people reach that freedom too."

"Is that why you killed her?" Michael uttered this question spontaneously. He hadn't planned it. It stunned him as the words poured out, but he fought to hide his surprise.

Theodorus looked at him as if it was the only response he expected from Michael.

"I didn't confess, Mr. Gate. In our previous conversation I said I had a choice to kill but that implies that I had an equal choice not to. Just as she had an equal choice to die or not to. I didn't confess then, and I have no intention of doing it now. You have to do a better job to break me down." Before Michael had time to respond, he continued. "And by the way, Mr. Rogers is growing his wings. I saw a peek of them when we were in the shower."

The last remark was bizarre, but bizarre had become one of Theodorus' trademarks. Michael felt tired but content as he let Theodorus go. He leaned back in his comfortable chair, closed his eyes for a second, and sent a wave of relaxation through his body the way he had for years.

A gentle smile touched his face. He liked being a psychiatrist. He felt recharged with new energy. He got up after a few minutes and before stepping out to the unit, he checked his pocket and touched something small and cold. It was the gold charm he had found in his garden. Upon closer investigation, it didn't seem as exquisite as he'd first thought. It clearly was something new, not antique, a fashionable piece, and utterly feminine. Michael looked at it with fascination. He knew no woman who would wear something like this. How bizarre to find this in his garden, he said to himself. The word *bizarre* immediately brought back the association with Theodorus. Michael felt certain this little heart was somehow connected with his patient. He couldn't explain that feeling rationally, but felt it strongly. He stood there indecisively, then put the charm back into his pocket and left his office.

15.

The curtain fell. There was silence in the room, hard to say for how long. Raphael would have claimed it lasted an eternity and yet it ended in a second. It ended in avalanche of applause and he suddenly realized how overwhelmed he was by his own creation, despite knowing all the slightest details of the production. The story had overpowered the form and claimed its life once again. The applause grew stronger, the success was palpable and Raphael knew he needed to escape before the flood of congratulations, hand-shakes, kisses, and hugs went his way. People started moving, getting up from their chairs, looking around nervously as if shaking off the confusion of returning to their routine world. Then they started talking, whispering at first as they moved out of the hall toward the exit, then speaking louder, more freely, then laughing and sharing their emotions with one another. Raphael walked through the theater rows following the exiting crowd. He was in a hurry.

He knew it would be difficult to find another person in the middle of the human cluster, but then he saw her shoulder in the silver coat. He recognized it by the pattern of unmistakable grace with which she made her way through throngs of people, her movements as precise as a scalpel cutting skin. She didn't push, didn't insist, she just moved purposefully, effortlessly, her left shoulder serving as tip of a ship navigating stormy water. Her hands moved around her as if protecting other people from accidental pushes. She was determined. And she got out fast. When he finally exited the main hall and saw her standing next to the column outside, writing something in her small notebook, Raphael didn't feel that he could approach her. She seemed protected by a wall of mystery. Her intensity was palpable.

She closed her notebook abruptly as she finished writing, slipped it into her little purse, and looked up to the sky. It was gray and heavy, the clouds pregnant with a late night rain. As the first drops began to reach the ground, people started running to their cars. She took out a cigarette and lit it, inhaled deeply as if trying to remember its taste. Raphael was stunned — he had never seen Nadia smoking. She took a few more puffs and then threw the cigarette to the wet ground. She pressed her blue shoe into the cigarette, and then waved to a cab. There was something cinematic in her figure, her outfit, the way she ran a few steps down to the cab under the rain, braving the bursts of wind and then pausing for a moment when another man opened the cab door for her.

Raphael watched it all happen from a distance in a fog of disappointment — they were supposed to have dinner after the opera.

He wanted so much to remember the man's face when the police interrogated him later. But the stranger had been obscured from his view and no matter how much he tried, Raphael couldn't recall any details. He could have told the police how he noticed changes in Nadia lately, how she, though always extremely private, had become even more secretive. How she had spent hours on the Internet and began to wear a strange, all-knowing smile on her face. But all he could remember in the end was standing there in the rain, oblivious to the flood of congratulations for the spectacular success of his opera, his eyes drawn to the last evidence of her — a squashed, wet cigarette butt that still carried a trace of her pearly lipstick.

Ignoring the rain and the soggy pats on the back from strangers, he walked over to the cigarette butt and picked it up, as if somehow he might protect her by keeping it safe. But as he looked at the rain-drenched cigarette, he knew it was too late. He had failed to protect her, he had failed to help her find peace. In fact, he had done the opposite — pushed her closer to some final decision through his opera, his gift to her.

He called the police the next day after she didn't return three of his messages. Because of his notoriety and connections, they opened a missing person investigation right away.

He never told the police about the cigarette.

16.

Artemis was standing next to her favorite tree. Her right foot in the golden sandal was tapping the grass gently and this is how Michael knew that she was losing her patience. They had spent the afternoon here, in the same place where they first met, having a conversation Michael had hoped to avoid.

"I need you, Michael," she said in her soft melodic voice. "Sometimes I need you more than you need me, even though you may never remember my call. But I always remember yours. And I will always answer it.

"I can see things the way you see them, but your eyes open to my world only when you are in your animal shape. Your daily mind is locked behind your fears and even though I know you carry my love inside, it kills me to realize that you have no memory of it, of us, of yourself loving me. You have to step over your fears and remember us. It will not make you less of a human; it will make you more, my love."

Michael felt a spasm clench his throat; it was hard for him to look at her — so fragile and yet so much stronger than him. What could he possibly give her that she didn't have? How could he possibly measure up to her greatness whether he was a human or an animal? It didn't matter, he was incomplete either way, and he felt weak.

"I am not worthy of your love." He still wouldn't look at her.

"Sometimes I think Maia with all her bitter judgment might be right." Artemis said it in a light-hearted way, but the words struck Michael profoundly, he almost felt angry with her for the first time.

"Come on, my love, don't be stubborn." She brushed his neck with her long fingers and his anger was instantly gone. No other woman in his life could pacify him as she could. He growled at her still, but lightly and playfully and everything was back to good.

"We still need to talk. Aren't you a shrink in your other life? Don't you talk for a living?" She was responding to his playful call but wouldn't let go of the topic. It always amazed him that she seemed to know everything about his other life.

"I always talk to you."

"Right, in that way a married man would talk to his mistress, with measured revelation and everything else off the table. Don't ask, don't tell. I actually like this comparison. I really do feel like a secret mistress."

"And who is my wife, then?" Michael asked, but as soon as he said it, he knew the answer.

"Why, you're married to your other life, of course. And you never want our paths to cross." She enjoyed playing with his guilt, whatever this guilt was coming from. Michael didn't know how to respond.

"Look, I am a Goddess for God's sake, I can't be reduced to a mistress, not for long, we have to change that." Her voice grew more serious and Michael realized he had no chance to avoid the discussion she decided to have today.

"Okay, let's talk." Michael tried to gather his professional focus but then realized quickly how ridiculous this scene was — here was a huge white wolf talking to a Goddess in the forest crowded with nymphs hiding behind the bushes, spying on them. He never could get rid of Artemis' entourage. He dropped his psychiatrist's pretense, sighed and looked straight at her, finally, ready to listen.

"Gods have been in love with humans since time immemorial, my love. Why do you think so many in your world feel so deeply that their soul mates are close, yet they can never find them? They just simply don't remember. The lover from another world is what destroys many of your kind. They can't remember because they don't allow themselves to. It's not like they don't want to remember the joy of love, they're just afraid to remember that part of themselves that's having this joy. Fear became bigger than pleasure for your kind. And so Gods suffer." Her light green eyes shone from her porcelain face as a sweet, warm wind toyed with her long black hair, dancing around her delicate yet unbelievably strong body.

"So what do you want me to do? I am just a mere human, a freak too, but still human." Michael felt hopeless and confused.

"Don't you ever call yourself a freak." Artemis sounded almost angry. "I gave you an incredible gift and you agreed to accept it, remember? Denial was never a part of it. I never asked you to forget. It was your 'rational' mind that put up the wall. How far is the denial in your other life going to take you? Do you realize that there is little difference between your pretension and the one that allows many of your patients to commit horrible crimes?"

"You are taking it too far." He couldn't believe she was serious.

"I am not taking it anywhere. I am keeping it right where it is, in front of your face to show you that the source of abuse and evildoing in your world originates in the denial of your own nature, more specifically, in the denial of the memories of what happened to you. Again I have to say, sometimes Maia is right, your people pretend all the time, to other people, to yourself, to your dreams."

"Well, if I am as hopeless as all my fellow humans, why don't you let me go then, why don't you find somebody stronger and more aware?" He sensed that little Mike, a lost little Mike, was talking now. He hardly could hold back the tears of resentment.

That didn't affect Artemis a bit.

"Because you made a choice and you made a promise; and because I love you. We have our bond and nobody is going to break it. But we need to work on it, and on ourselves."

"What can I do to become more aware?" he asked in a quiet voice, sincerely.

"Come with me. I want to show you something."

Michael got up and followed her, no questions asked. He felt tired but somehow resolved. Instead of running, they walked side by side, a gracious Goddess and her wolf-lover. They walked in unity and synchronicity and all the curious nymphs that were hiding in surrounding bushes followed, running from tree to tree, trying to stay hidden, only their melodic, child-like voices betraying their proximity.

The sun was setting when they reached the other end of the forest and walked into a small field. The field was covered with strange, yellow flowers. Michael couldn't recall their name but he remembered seeing them before. They resembled daisies, but with fewer petals. They undulated in the wind, row upon row as though somebody's careful hand had planted them there on purpose.

The trees surrounding the field seemed content to have stopped growing so that the sun might shine on the flowers throughout the day. A spring running along the edge of the field fed the flowers as a mother tending her children. There was something else about the spring — something that captured Michael's heart when he saw it. He slowed his steps, accepting his hunting stance and moving toward it with all caution, the way he might approach any live creature.

It wasn't the smell that made the spring different. There was no smell. And it wasn't its sound, even though the water's flow sounded remarkably similar to a woman's cry. It was something else about this spring that made Michael's hair stand up. He couldn't take his eyes off the water. For a moment, he forgot about Artemis, the first time that had ever happened in the forest.

He needed to remember something desperately, but couldn't, something that was intimately connected to this spring, something that was the spring itself, something he knew from before. His muscles ached from the tension, his teeth clenched, and he could almost see a woman's hands reaching out to him from under the water, from the depth of the spring, as if somebody were crying out for help.

"She is here," Artemis said behind his back. Michael felt a shiver go down to his bones. He was afraid to ask who she was.

He didn't have to say it out loud. Artemis knew. She remained behind him, giving him privacy to feel everything without distraction.

"The woman with the letters," she said softly and the spring cried out, splashing Michael's face. He felt dizzy. In his heart of hearts, he knew it was his purpose to find her, and to help her, and here she was. And he had no idea what to do about it.

"Okay Michael, enough drama." Artemis stood right in front of him. "I turned her into this spring," she said, and when she saw the horror on Michael's face she added quickly, "temporarily, of course. The moment she appeared here, everybody tried to help her. Her story was whispered around and spread like a fire and very soon there was not a creature in the woods that didn't know about her and her love. Yet she couldn't see anything. She wandered this meadow for days. That's what a strong human mind can do — it can create incredible resolve and conviction and it can also lock you stubbornly in a little circle of your own expectations."

Like a child's train, thought Michael.

Artemis continued. "Her expectation that her lover would be waiting for her here was so strong and fixed that when she finally realized he wasn't rushing to meet her, she got stuck in her grief again with a conviction I've rarely seen before. She would walk in circles, day and night, crying, inconsolable. Heartbreaking.... That was what my nymphs told me after they had tried, unsuccessfully, to reach her and to comfort her with their songs and dance, with their gentle little touches. She couldn't see or feel anything but her pain. The irony of it is that he *is* waiting for her here. But his perception, too, is limited. He is not a God, he is still a human in transition, even though he is wise and patient. But she has to find her way to him before they can see each other again. So I turned her into the spring... temporarily. She is still crying all her tears but it is much less distressing for everybody."

The spring water ran calmly now, as if the woman beneath it had heard their conversation and it changed her. Michael tried to make sense of the emotions he felt as he listened to Artemis but it was too much; there were no words to describe the overwhelming compassion and connection he felt with this woman and her story. It was intimately personal. She had given up her human form and existence to be with the one she loved. Michael had been doing the same for many years. Until this moment, he had always felt alone in his transformation; he did feel like a freak because nobody else knew what it was like to feel love that extends way beyond the human existence. But this woman did and he felt tremendous kinship with her.

"What can I do to help her? I feel that there is something I am supposed to do for her. Isn't it why you brought me here?" He turned to Artemis.

"It is not only her pain that holds her here. She is nearly ready to let that go. But there are other things that need to happen before she can move on. Her name in your world needs to have closure. That can't happen until her case is closed so people stop looking for her. It is not about the ritual, not at all. It is about her psyche and her way of knowing herself that is very much based on her memory of her body. When she feels at peace that her former existence was taken care of and that her disappearance causes no more distress for anybody, she will restore her complete memory of herself and she will be able to return to her lover. You are the only one who can help with that."

Artemis paused for a second; the gentle wind swung her long hair around her face so Michael couldn't see the look on it, but he almost sensed her smiling.

"Nobody stays in limbo forever, Michael. Nobody."

He felt a metallic taste in his mouth, familiar from childhood; he experienced it every time in his human reality when he was about to cry. He traced it to one particular day when as a little kid he tried to lick a metal stick in his backyard in the middle of the winter and his tongue stuck to the hot-frozen metal. A mix of fear and helplessness had pushed him to tears then, and now he experienced it here, in this reality. The emotion was so strong it triggered the transformation. The wind blew stronger, her face faded, and all the sounds muted and mixed into one deep vibration. But before it was over, in the middle of his transition when he couldn't identify whether he was still an animal or already a human, a deep thought hit him like a twister: *I am in limbo and I can't stay here forever. If I don't remember, I am going to lose her....*

Michael awoke in his bed, his pillow wet, metal taste in his mouth, and he realized that he was crying. Try as he might, he couldn't remember the dream. All he could feel was the urge to remember something as if his life depended on it.

But what was it?

17.

One week later Michael came to work an hour early. He had awakened before his alarm went off, to the beautiful sunlit morning, and the sound of birds singing in his garden. Michael looked forward to this day for he felt it was going to be a particularly good one. When he arrived at the hospital, it was still early and while he'd expected the halls to be empty, they seemed too quiet. His gut suddenly wrenched like never before and he knew instantly that something bad, something really, really bad had happened. He didn't rush his steps through the hall though. People walking toward him looked preoccupied with their daily routines, nothing in their appearances screamed emergency. Yet Michael's legs felt like they were made of lead as he forced his steps toward his unit.

The internal panic became nauseating. When he saw a red light, not blinking but solid, over the entrance to his unit, he knew his gut feeling was right. As he slowed, he saw a cart and an emergency crew surrounding a body lying on the cart. It was clear they were performing a resuscitation. Michael couldn't see the face of a person, but he saw that he was dressed in hospital uniform so he knew it was one of the patients. The nurse from his unit saw him and rushed to update Michael on what exactly had taken place.

"We found him in a day room just a few moments ago. Actually, Mr. Rogers saw him dropping dead and alerted us so we called for an emergency crew. It's kind of a miracle Mr. Rogers had stayed on the unit — everyone else had gone to the cafeteria — otherwise we may have not known until it was too late. Of course, it could be..."

The nurse couldn't finish her sentence. The hospital staff was used to fights, violence, rage, but not medical emergencies; most of the incarcerated men were in good physical shape.

"Who is it?" Michael felt a momentary flush of relief when he realized it wasn't violence that brought the emergency crew, but rather a medical emergency. Probably a heart attack, he thought.

"Mr. Theodorus," the nurse said casually, and Michael felt as if he had been punched in the stomach.

He walked up to the cart to see Theodorus' body lying stretched on the carrier, lifeless, unresponsive. The crew alternated CPR rounds, performing every step precisely as if his body were a practice mannequin. Michael had become so used to having this man's observant presence around that it felt unreal not to be under the radar of his penetrating eyes, not to sense the judging sharpness of his ever-sarcastic mind.

"What's the prognosis?" Michael asked one of the crewmembers.

"Doesn't look good, Doc. We are going to roll him into the medical floor, our Doc is on the way but so far he is unresponsive. We don't have much time left."

In coordinated efforts they started the cart and, while somebody still performed CPR, they drove away with a flashing red light and siren through the hospital hall toward the medical unit. Michael stepped into his office. Everything was business as usual. Patients were returning from breakfast. Groups were about to start. Medications were distributed. Nothing seemed out of order. Yet Michael felt more panicky with every passing moment. Technically, there was nothing he could do. The medical and psychiatric services were strictly separate, and both were top tier. Everything was going according to procedure. The emergency response was generated on time, help had arrived, the protocol worked like a clock, yet Michael's rational mind couldn't find a way to calm down his panic.

Protocol and order are not enough, thought Michael. He felt a strange urge. A pushing feeling that he must do something to save his patient's life and that "something," whatever it was, kept turning his guts inside-out. There was no protocol for this feeling. Michael stopped fighting his impulse, left his office, and walked straight to the medical floor.

The resuscitation efforts continued there. Monitoring machines were hooked now to Theodorus' lifeless body, projecting one straight line after another on the screen with merciless precision. Everything looked final, static, solid, irreversible — the man's body on a stretcher, cold, heavy, eyes closed, no visible breathing, color of his cheeks even more greenish-gray under the daylight lamp placed above his face. The emergency team continued performing CPR but one could tell that they had given up by how mechanical their actions had become.

Michael stood at the head of the stretcher. The medical doctor saw him and acknowledged him with a head nod; he was busy orchestrating his team's work. Michael studied the man's face, noticing how the decision to end the resuscitation was shaping in his mind. Time had begun to slow. Michael could observe and process every slight detail of what was happening.

The next moment, the doctor stopped, looked at the monitors and said in a very tired voice, "Stop it, he is gone." His crew obeyed instantly. Someone began to remove the IVs, another person shut off the monitors. The protocol for ending life was as precise and routine as the one for preserving it. Michael didn't move. He felt no emotion, his mind was clear, his heartbeat was regular, and nobody who saw him would notice anything unusual.

Yet, something very different was happening inside of him.

He couldn't accept this scenario. There was a different possible ending. There had to be. He felt strongly that he couldn't conform to the current version of reality and the feeling of disagreement grew so intense that it overtook all other perceptions. Michael started feeling as if he were flying over the ground. He knew he was still standing at the head of Theodorus' lifeless body, yet his mind jumped above it as if the air were some kind of penetrable fabric. It bent and stretched and then opened up under the force of Michael's intention and he found himself in a separate reality that appeared in the same physical space but connected only through Michael's mind. He felt overwhelmed but focused. There were noises, movements, presences surrounding him, yet he knew he didn't have the energy and capacity to pay full attention to them.

"He can't die," he said in his mind, directing his words into the center of this new reality, feeling confident that there was somebody out there who could reverse the outcome.

"Why not?" the short, sharp answer came from that center and Michael perceived it in his mind.

"Because I simply can't allow it to happen."

"So what are you going to do about it?"

Michael didn't have time to think — more precisely he couldn't think in a way he was used to, linear thinking didn't exist in this new reality, for everything there was multi-dimensional. Michael was about to cry, like a little child who feels powerless to explain a point to adults because he doesn't understand their language. A white wolf, beautiful, strong, full of life ran in front of Michael as if showing him his way. Michael was struck by the sense of connection and familiarity this animal caused in him. His heart burst into millions of pieces and yet it remained whole and strong.

"Whatever you tell me to do to reverse this."

"Fair enough," the voice said from the center of the overwhelming reality. "If you can love him enough, he can stay."

Michael looked at Theodorus' face from above. All other noises, images, distractions subsided. He knew exactly what he had been requested to do.

Michael focused his eyes on his patient's face. He knew that love couldn't be forced, nor could it be altered or suppressed. It just existed there as a universal force, bigger than any individual being, encompassing and penetrating every single one of them whether they were aware of it or not.

Michael knew that he needed to focus all the energy of love flowing freely through him at Theodorus. He looked at his patient's face and contemplated it for a moment. His features were so known and familiar — way beyond the personal interaction they had experienced as doctor and patient. In that moment, Michael knew this was the most dear, precious, and beloved face of another human being. He let himself feel this emotion without reservation, for he felt it was changing something radically in him as well. The wolf circled in front of him as if dancing. Behind the majestic creature, he watched tall trees blowing gently in the breeze. A woman's voice laughed — so close he felt she was inside of him. "You did it, my love," the voice whispered, and then he remembered.

He remembered everything — her beauty, his love, their life together inside the universe of myriads of possibilities. All of it came to him in an instant and all the bridges to oblivion burned and fell and there was no way back to the life of denial after that.

"Artemis." He said her name, said it for the first time as a human and it felt as if the whole universe burst into laughter.

Theodorus' body convulsed violently and he suddenly sat up. His eyes were still closed, needles still sticking out of his veins. His muscles contracted with immense force and he started howling like a wolf. His face turned up to the ceiling and he howled in a deep, animal, primal voice, freezing everyone in the room. The technicians stopped, the nurses turned and watched him in horror, and the doctor, his hand holding a pen above the death certificate, gasped as if he'd seen a ghost.

Theodorus' body convulsed again and he made another deep howling sound. Then the doctor jumped to his feet and commanded, "He's back and he's having a seizure, put his IVs back on!" The emergency crew jumped to life again, as if the brief interruption in reality had been cured by the doctor's decree. Michael smiled and stepped back. He stood there for a moment, not because he felt he was needed anymore, his work was done. He paused before taking a step back to the hall. The pause was short. He didn't need any preparation. It was so easy and natural to finally be himself, just the way he always wanted to be.

He returned to his office and took out his notebook. When he reached into his pocket to get his monogrammed pen, he found the gold charm. The little heart with the diamond in the center shined so brightly in the daylight. Michael held it in his open palm and looked at it as if it were the most precious object he had ever seen. Tears came to his eyes and he remembered. It struck him in the heart how interconnected everything was, and how beautiful. This little heart in the middle of his palm pulsated in the center of the universe and connected all other hearts, including his. He knew that Theodorus would be okay now.

Michael put the heart back into his pocket, took a pen, and wrote something in his notebook, smiling with pleasure, thinking about a phone call he was about to make to the DA. As he reached for the phone, Michael recalled his most recent experience in the forest. The memory returned to him with such clarity that he felt as if he were experiencing it all over again.

18.

The road was narrow and passed through the center of the meadow. Michael didn't hurry; he padded slowly through the tall, juicy grass, his soft paws bouncing, his body striding forward effortlessly. He was acutely aware of himself and in complete command of his wolf-body's functions, yet part of him was separated from it. Pretension lingered in the back of his mind as his large, muscled, fur-covered frame made its way through this altered reality. It was only when he was with Artemis that all the walls in his mind collapsed; bodies didn't matter when they merged, intertwined, melted together. They could accept any shape and create any form — they could be wolves, birds, plants, people, Gods, and in fact they were all of those things in one when they were making love to each other.

He had been circling the forest for days. He hadn't seen Artemis since she'd shown him the spring. She was giving all the time he needed to accomplish his task. Michael hardly knew what his task was except that he had to find something that could release Nadia from her limbo. Michael focused on trying to find the place she went with Theodorus after the opera. But he had no clues. Every time he went through the transformation back to his human form, he tried to re-member this question so Michael, the psychiatrist might gather some clues from Theodorus. Michael the psychiatrist had no memory of this realm beyond its existence, and no way of knowing what Artemis had asked him to do. So in wolf form, Michael only had instinct to guide him.

His instinct was strong, but trusting it was no easy task. He had to run for hours sometimes, just to calm his fear of losing Artemis should he fail to help Nadia. Today he ran, and he ran, and ran again. Despite the unassailable anxiety, he still enjoyed it. To match his body's tremendous movement with awareness was a pleasure he had never dreamed of before. Running in this reality felt as if all the cells in his body sang a melody of joy from being recognized by him, the master of this body, and there was no rejection.

Suddenly he stopped, shocked by the smell of the river before he could see or hear it. In this world a river wasn't just a body of water moving steadily and passively in one direction, it was also a powerful entity that breathed and danced and kept secrets — secrets he could smell. Scent was his dictionary and it was extensive beyond belief and it continued to expand with each new smell he encountered. It was a library without words, but full of unique patterns of life.

The river ahead smelled fruity, with a deep, dark, sweet, and alarming sense of something that had crossed from here for good. It was an old smell but it alarmed him with new force. Michael stopped briefly to gather his strength for he knew he was finally onto something. When he moved closer to the source, Michael could see that the river was long gone, yet the canyon where it used to be still carried the smell of it. Michael came closer and looked around. The full moon shone bright and he could see his surroundings clearly.

The uneven bottom of the dry creek was covered with rocks, dead tree branches, some trash. The walls were concrete and there was a large aluminum tube running down the pass on its right side. It was peaceful here. The wind cried through the canyon, accompanied by an occasional loud siren and the sound of a truck speeding by the nearby freeway.

The freeway. This was familiar to Michael. He looked for it, but the freeway was clearly behind some invisible boundary. It was here and it was somewhere else at the same time, the two realities coming into contact at their edges in this canyon, but never truly crossing each other.

He observed a gas station nearby with some bikers still hanging around even though it was the middle of the night. They didn't notice Michael when he ran through the canyon. An old warehouse with a large, almost washed-off sign, "Antique Depot," filled the space in the open field across from the gas station. Michael paused his determined run to take in all the energy coming from the warehouse. He smelled a diverse and almost overwhelming collection of history inside those tall, wooden walls — china dolls with long, lowered eyelashes, dressed in lace dresses and little satin shoes, grand mirrors in heavy golden frames that had become heavier with each image they captured over the years, beautiful jewelry — gold, silver, diamonds — owned by rich and powerful people of the past, waiting patiently to be found by a new master so that their beauty could grace the world again. Michael allowed himself to inhale this energy of the past before continuing over the canyon. He really loved antiques.

He saw the shack almost immediately, on the other side of the canyon. It was an old place abandoned long ago. But it was not empty. Not tonight. The scent coming from the house was so strong that it overpowered all the energy that Michael had gathered from the antique place. Something had happened in the house and not long ago.

Michael stopped at the bottom of the old creek. He looked around. The occasional creaking of a branch under a burst of wind was the only sound in this place at this hour. Michael walked slowly up the side of the canyon until he could see the whole house from under the bushes.

There was no light inside but Michael could see all the smallest details vividly under the glow of the full moon. Two wooden benches sat under each window, colored with similar dark green paint. The benches looked heavy and worn. It was strange to imagine anybody ever sitting there. A large oak tree grew too close to the house and its large branches blocked the windows. During the daytime the house and its insides would always be covered in the shadow. One of the tree branches, the largest one, had an old, fraying hammock attached to it, but only on one side, the other side had fallen long ago. The hammock just hung there with one side fixed to the tree and the other dragging along the ground, waving in the wind like some old, thick, forgotten spider web.

The shack was in ruins, and as Michael approached he could see every evidence of its decay. He didn't have to push the door open; it was half-open already, moving slightly in the wind. The rafters in the wooden roof had fallen, exposing the starry sky through an opening in the ceiling. Yet the wind remained outside the battered building and it was silent and calm inside.

Nadia had been here not so long ago. Michael saw her silver coat glittering under the moonlight as it hung casually across the back of an old rocking chair. It looked as if she left it there just a moment ago, the rocking chair looked as if it could have stopped rocking only a moment earlier. But he knew it had been still for months.

Michael looked around carefully. His ears moved back and forth, two antennas, checking out the space all around. Silence was in such abundance that it was ready to burst. Michael sniffed the air searching for scents that might be clues. The interior had no smell — even the strong scent that guided Michael was not allowed inside.

But there was plenty to see. Even though it was dark, all the objects were well outlined and visible as if glowing.

Michael shook his body violently as the fur began to rise and he felt a deep, strong desire to howl. He suppressed that desire. Michael, the man, knew how to deal with fears and dangerous situations. He called upon that wisdom and it calmed him. He began to observe the details in the room. The rocking chair, a dining table without any chairs, and a massive black bookcase still protecting a few books under a thick layer of dust. The bookcase stood in the corner and was the only object in the room not lit by moonlight. Suddenly the bookcase made a creaking sound and Michael jumped to face it as alert as ever. A large, jet-black crow sat on the top of the bookcase, and by the look of its beady eyes, Michael knew it was the same bird that visited his garden.

The crow broke the silence.

"Strange how human nature runs underneath your wolf's blood, doubt seated so deep in you I wouldn't have even guessed it was there if it wasn't for the perfection of my vision."

"Well, hello to you too." Michael didn't have to voice his words, their communication was telepathic. He decided to take charge of this communication right away, for it already showed signs of going wrong. Michael needed information. "So where is her body?" he asked the crow without waiting for him to respond.

The crow sat there silently for a while and then answered: "So you want to reconcile the past, future, and the now, I reckon? Then of course you need the body. But look around; the body is nowhere to be found.... Just the shoes, the coat, and the purse. So goes the time continuum — nowhere to be found, annihilated, non-existent. Welcome to the nonlinear, my friend. And don't flatter yourself thinking that I dropped the gold heart in your garden to lead your way, I was just looking for a place to hide my treasure. Your garden seemed like the perfect spot. The real question is why I dropped the treasure before I could hide it? That may be the answer in your favor. Flatter yourself with that."

"Where is the body?" Michael repeated, resolved to get all the information he needed no matter the cost. The exchange would be unpleasant, words or no words. This crow was stubborn.

"I just told you, stupid. The body is nowhere to be found. Does it mean anything to you?" The crow's response came to Michael as a sharp arrow.

"It means the body is hidden, obviously. And don't call me stupid." Michael's fur was on end again. He froze in his posture, waiting for the anger to pass.

"Then stop being stupid, and listen to what I have to say. 'Nowhere' doesn't mean 'hidden somewhere,' it means nowhere. Not here, not there, not anywhere."

"How is that possible?"

"Really? Did you just ask me that question? And a moment ago you asked me not to call you stupid? Can't do that. Because if you were not stupid you would have understood by now that the body simply doesn't exist any more."

"How do you know?"

"I was here."

"So it happened here, in this house? Was anybody else with her?"

"What are you going to give me if I answer your questions?"

"The gold heart with diamonds you dropped in my house." Michael wasn't bluffing, he still had it.

"It is not yours to give."

"As it is not yours to take." Michael had an advantage now as the bird's obsession with gold became obvious.

"Okkkay," the crow cawed. "Listen to this story, but listen very, very carefully, because this story is not simple to verify."

"What on earth do you mean by that?"

"By that I mean, first and foremost, don't interrupt, ignorant creature, and the knowledge will be yours."

It would be impossible for one to look more pompous and grandiose at this moment than the crow sitting on the corner of the old bookshelf. Michael laughed to himself, picturing the bird accidentally losing balance for being so inflated and falling to the ground. It would have been spectacular. But that didn't happen and the crow continued.

"She suffered greatly, in her mind she did. I don't have to be a psychiatrist to see that she was punishing herself and burdened with guilt that she wasn't even aware of."

Michael fought the urge to snap back at the psychiatrist dig. Instead he just sat on the floor and kept listening.

The crow made a dramatic pause and continued: "She invested everything into her love; it was her salvation, her escape, her never-born child, and her triumph. There was nothing she wouldn't do for that love. And she had done everything — believe me she had — she had lied, she had cheated, she was ready to destroy other people, just to be with her beloved. And it was all worth it. The role guilt played was minor, it was all about her father — she lost him early in life — but the child's imagined guilt, led her to something greater. Indeed, it was a great love, one that happens only in a few hundred years. Only a few can sustain the task of handling a love like this, for it can burn like hell, it can enslave you, it becomes an ultimate dictator in your life and yet, you wouldn't want it any other way.

"Of course she couldn't go on in the world without love. She became like a dog that couldn't go on after losing its master. She was that dog and love was her leash and it led her straight to this abandoned place. Of course she was helped and guided."

Michael's ears moved to the side, he was all attention, awaiting the most important revelation to come.

"The powers from beyond human regulations arranged for her this channel and transition."

"Do you want the gold or not?" Michael couldn't stop the irritation after the glimpse of hope disappeared with the crow's last sentence.

"You ignorant fool!" The crow looked around with obvious tension, "how dare you dismiss the greatest secret that I was about to bestow upon you?"

"Just answer the question, yes or no, and if it is still yes, let me ask you what I want to know."

The crow sat silently for while, thinking, and then said in a raspy voice, "Shoot your questions," and after a pause added with utmost sarcasm, "Doc."

"Did she come here by herself?"

"Yes and no."

Michael shot him a look.

"Okay, no. But it is all so relative, it can't be seen as black and white. Okay, okay, you win. The Messenger was here with her, but you already know that."

"The Messenger?"

"Messenger Theodorus."

Michael got very attentive now. "And?"

"She found him on the Internet, through the agency. And he did what he was supposed to do. He guided her here, he assisted her with the transformation, and after it was done he went on to find somebody who would complete the circle. That would be you."

"What exactly was done?"

"The transformation."

"What kind?"

"The kind that you do all the time, only in her case she didn't change into anything quite so smelly as a wolf. She just got naked, smeared on some body cream Theodorus provided, took a map and some instructions from him, then sat on a broom and flew out the window. In her case it was a one-way ticket. She is not coming back to pick up her stuff from here any time soon, or should I say anytime ever."

"Do you mean she was killed?"

"I'm thinking I might just have to call you stupid again. Really, Doc? You are not getting killed and resurrected every time you shape-shift, are you? Why would she?"

"So there was no crime involved?"

"Precisely."

"So where is her body now?"

"Where is your psychiatrist's body now?"

This caught Michael by surprise, he had never asked himself that question.

"Exactly," the crow continued, "and as I have said already the body is nowhere to be found."

"So how can this case have closure if there is no body?"

The crow laughed out loud. "I thought you worked in the state system. Didn't they teach you anything about bureaucracy? All you need is a piece of paper from her telling them that she is okay and that no crime happened. It's all about the right piece of paper in the system, you know. That paper is still in her purse. All you need to do is just give them this location. And then she will be free."

Michael sat in silence for a while. Something almost trivial prompted his next question.

"So you can order a transformation like this on the Internet? Through the agency?"

The crow turned his head to the side and gave Michael a long look as if there were no words worthy of answering this nonsense.

"Come on already, bird, just tell me." Michael's patience was reaching its limit.

"Of course that's not what she requested. She initially looked for some other means to end her pain, assisted suicide or something like that. But how often do humans truly know what they are asking for when they are asking for something?"

"Huh?"

"That's the human predicament. Humans play this game of pretending to not be aware and not remember, and they truly believe that. But who am I telling this to? A couple more hours and you are back in that game yourself, not a trace of any memory as if this conversation never happened. She was human, she was no exception, she had her fantasies, you know."

"You mentioned some cream. What kind of cream did he give her?"

"Vaseline. So she could fly."

"Vaseline, so she could fly?"

"Vaseline, that ancient, magical potion, the power of which is so unfortunately underappreciated."

"Can you cut your crap please, and explain what you mean."

"No, it really was Vaseline." The crow instantly dropped his sarcasm. His mood shifted so unpredictably from one extreme to another that it gave a theatrical flavor to everything he said, even when he was simple and serious.

"It was a placebo. A placebo, by the way, is the most powerful drug humans have. It fed her imagination since she was so entranced with the story of *The Master and Margarita*. She was given it to repeat the transformation she envisioned powerfully so many times by following the story of Margarita. It was enough to give her Vaseline so she might allow herself to fly. In reality, she could have easily sat in this rocking chair and rocked herself to the same transformation, or danced herself out of here, or sang... it doesn't matter. The form serves the conditioning. But it is not essential. The transformation is all the same anyways, like yours. You think you turn into a wolf, she thought she turned into a witch who could fly. Both things are true and both things are the same."

"So are you saying bodies don't matter?"

The crow shook its head, a look of exasperation in its beady eyes.

"You are not your body whatever body you have. That is all I have to say for today. Now how are you going to give me my treasure? Is it still in your house?"

"I will leave it in the garden for you by tomorrow morning."

"How are you going to remember about it in the morning? Your human addiction to denial is pretty severe."

"Addiction?"

"Precisely. Denial is one of the most powerful addictions. In your case it's so bad that you should probably sign up for Deniers Anonymous. Oh, wait, there is none, because people are so attached to their precious denials that they would rather die than give them up. But don't worry, I'm going to plant the seed of moral responsibility into your psychiatric head so it will stay with you and trouble you and eventually help you to get out of your denial so you can leave my treasure by the statue."

"How exactly are you going to plant that seed?"

"I just did," and then without explaining he changed the topic. "And by the way, the omnipresent love that she had experienced and that she thought was the ultimate goal of her life is available for anyone. Know what else? It's not even that ultimate. What she had experienced was just a glimpse of how things are in the universe. We crows know this deeper than any other species. Do you want to know why? When you're talking to me, you are seeing only one face of the whole crowhood, I am one part of the totality and I am totally aware of it, pardon my redundancy. When one of us experiences something, the whole crowhood experiences it and becomes instantly aware of it. Any individual experience is recorded in the collective memory of crows available for everybody. This is how it is going to be for other species when they evolve to our level. But you are not able to comprehend this yet, not as a wolf because you haven't found your pack, and surely not as a confused man, that species will take much longer to reach a point of connectedness. She was ahead of her tribe as a human, though not exceptional. It made a fun story though."

Having said that the crow suddenly took off and flew out of the door without another word. Michael watched him go and before he had a chance to process this whole encounter the ground beneath him started shaking. The last thing he remembered before the wave struck his muscles was the faces from the antique photographs, and the deep sadness and closeness he felt with those strangers from the past.

Humans are my pack and we are much closer than we believe.

The thought crossed his mind and then his vision narrowed as he passed back into his other existence....

Michael smiled, sitting in his office, as he remembered the encounter with the crow. His newly felt connectedness with the world outside and with his own memories felt sweet and profound. Michael remembered the gas station and the antique store next to it and he realized that he knew exactly where the shack was located. Now it was only a matter of formalities.

19.

A distant bell sounded from the other side of the hill. A new scent reached his nostrils. Soon the sound of galloping became apparent but there was something odd about the approaching horses, something Michael had never experienced before. He had seen a few horses in the forest, they sensed him from afar, he would hear their neighing before seeing them, and he would smell the anguished fear that even the anticipation of his presence revealed in them. But the horses approaching from behind the hill were different, different in a way that made Michael, the wolf, step back, his fur raised, his nostrils flattened, his instincts alarmed. The field around the house silenced. The birds stopped singing. The wind stopped caressing the green grass and flowering bushes and even the clouds in the sky refused to move. Everything waited for what was about to come. Michael hid behind a large bush, next to the wall of the house. He was safe there and yet he could see and hear everything.

The galloping approached and its sound together with the bells made a complete rhythmic melody, so cheerful and pleasant, it was hard not to smile hearing it. The door of the house opened with a small creaking sound, the same way it opened every day at this dawn hour, and Michael saw the man walk out onto the porch. He had witnessed the same event so very often but only now realized what was so different about the man. He never communicated with his environment, he watched it all, he smiled, he followed clouds with his eyes, he enjoyed the warmth of the evening sun touching his skin, but he never presented himself to this reality as somebody who could be seen, perceived, approached. It was almost like he couldn't remember. He was just waiting, and that was all that he remembered about himself.

Three white horses bridled into a golden carriage emerged from behind the hill. Their horseshoes didn't touch the ground, yet they were galloping through the field, strong, joyful, and determined until they stopped, in perfect harmony, in front of the main entrance.

There was no horseman, the troika was special and that was obvious. The man walked down the porch steps toward the carriage. His face changed profoundly with every step he made, it became more awake, more present, and more aware. Before he reached the ground, the door of the carriage shot open and a woman jumped to the ground. She saw him right away. There still was some distance separating them and she ran toward him as he stopped and stood still, watching her.

The woman had an unbelievable grace, running in high heeled blue shoes with little gold hearts sparkling around her ankles, silver coat flowing behind her. She was in ecstasy. Michael watched brilliant tears roll down her face like diamonds, covering it and blending happiness and pain into one powerful emotion and that emotion was love. He remained transfixed as the miraculous alchemy of memory and love transformed these two people from separate, lost, incomplete beings into one entity. When the woman gently touched his hand and then his face, she spoke something to him softly, his name; the miracle was complete. The man remembered who he was and the reality around them transformed in an instant. The lights went on in the house, the sound of piano and laughing voices poured out from an open window, boys from the nearby village appeared carrying baskets of food and wine, and the horseman who finally appeared lovingly but firmly walked the horses to the stable.

"You are so beautiful, my love," the man said as he touched the woman's face and wiped her tears with his hand. Then he added with his kind smile, "You've suffered so much, so much my poor one. But the suffering is over for us. Come with me. We have a party to attend. I think our guests have been waiting for us for a while."

She smiled and put her hand under his arm. As they walked toward the door, everything began to move again, the grass under the wind, the clouds in the sky, the sound of laughter and piano playing from the house. The world awoke.

The lump in Michael's throat he remembered from human experience but had never felt in his animal shape; but it didn't last long. The lump started pulsating, the overwhelming emotions channeled themselves into pure energy, twisting his muscles, pushing his consciousness into the familiar narrow corridor and he was gone from here faster than ever, back to the world of humans where he still belonged.

20.

The sun was going down and the place looked exactly like it did the first time he met Artemis under this tree. He couldn't say how much time had passed since then — eternity or nothing, or more precisely, both. She had become his eternity and time with her was one never-ending moment.

She stood under the tree, its soft leaves touching the golden silk of the tunic on her shoulders. She squinted and her eyes looked even greener and more sparkly. Michael walked toward her, his eyes lost in hers. The contact was so palpable, so comfortable and deep that he forgot everything else around him. Artemis smiled and turned away a little as if pointing out something to him.

He looked around, nobody in sight; even her nymphs seemed to be away and not just hiding. He tried to catch her eyes again but she still faced away and all he could see was her lingering half-smile. Michael walked closer and the revelation struck him as lightning, knocking him from the ground he was standing on. He looked at Artemis as a man and as a wolf at the same time, there was no separation. And in that lightning flash, he realized he could be whomever he wanted to be — that all of his transformations would only empower who he truly was, without taking anything away. He experienced in that flash the presence of his true self, always relaxed, happy and aware of any identities, thoughts, and feelings he was experiencing in the moment. Michael could be a bird, a panther, a woman, or any other man, and still be himself.

He became that squinted eye behind the bullet. There was no destruction, no end, and no more denial.

He realized that she would still love him, no matter how much he would change. He walked up to Artemis and she turned to him. Of course she knew what was happening inside of him. She looked at Michael with love and connection unparalleled to everything he had ever experienced. He touched her raven black hair, caressed it gently, and then slowly and so tenderly kissed her forehead; he felt it, stayed with it, drank the feeling in and still there was no bottom to it.

"At the beginning there was Happiness, my love," she said softly. "Only then came the Word, and it changed everything. The Word said that Happiness was lost, but in truth it was just a game of words, because Happiness didn't go anywhere. But when Word created the illusion of paradise lost, we all had to create Love - all of us - Gods, humans, Forces, so we could experience it again, come back full circle, back to the primordial Happiness we never truly lost. But the journey was worth it for now we have Love with us and she makes Happiness even sweeter.

"This is why humans are so precious to immortal Gods. Because humans die they have learned to nurture Love. And that makes love so much sweeter."

Michael listened and he understood.

She continued, "And we Gods are precious to you because our perception of you shapes who you are."

"Who do you perceive me to be now?" Michael smiled and he felt so relaxed. It took him notable effort to keep the conversation going, for more than anything he just wanted to dissolve in her.

"You are a wolf that dreams, Michael. Sometimes you dream you are human. But more importantly, you are me," she whispered gently. She moved back a little and then pulled herself toward him looking for his lips with her own. Just before they kissed, he closed his eyes and smiled. In the next moment when he gave himself completely to her, he knew exactly what she meant.

21.

Michael tried to prepare himself for this meeting. He knew it would be their last. All the paperwork was signed and admitted to the court. The decision had been made. Theodorus was declared competent and ready to return to jail. In light of the new information, the DA was inclined to dismiss charges against him and most likely he would be sent home to wait for the closure. But Michael knew something else.

He had called the cardiologist in care of Theodorus when he was transferred to ICU and his prognosis looked gray. The doctor told Michael that he "had never seen anybody survive a heart attack like this, it's probably as close to a miracle as I ever got." The myocardial infarction involved the total cardiac muscle and even though Theodorus had miraculously survived it, it was only a matter of months if not days before his heart would give up for good. Michael didn't want to feel emotional, but the experience at Theodorus' clinical death still echoed as powerfully now as when it happened.

Theodorus was being returned to the psychiatric hospital for discharge. It was 10 in the morning when the nurse called Michael to inform him that the patient had arrived. Michael paused before going to meet his patient, attempting to embrace the fundamental change that had taken place in his world since he last saw Theodorus.

"People used to compare somebody like me to an animal..." he remembered Theodorus saying at one of their meetings. Too often his patients were subjected to that comparison. From his new understanding, he realized that this was unfair — to the animals, of course. So was calling them predators. True, they were like animals, to some extent, but wounded, scared, terrified animals striking out of pain and fear. The true predator was within oneself, he thought. One becomes predator against himself when the mind commits crimes against the heart, when one suppresses what he feels, one's nature, one's memory, when one preys against one's own nature. It's only when we are ready to break through our own denial that we become an animal, one who loves, one who can feel love and who can share it, without fear.

It was also evident now how prone to prejudice Michael's mind was. He had judged Theodorus based on past crimes for which he had served his time. Michael had expected him to be a malicious, game-loving psychopath just because of the history he carried. He didn't feel surprised, but rather disappointed in himself. After years of working he should have known better.

Michael walked downstairs to the admission suite and saw Theodorus before his patient could see him. He sat in a wheelchair, facing the large window with green hills outside. Slowly he turned to face Michael standing at the door.

"Good to see you, Dr. Gate." His voice was soft but still strong and he smiled genuinely.

"Same here." Michael's voice cracked from the emotional pressure and he didn't try to hide it. He was just happy to see his patient.

Theodorus looked paler than usual, and thinner, his long gray hair tied up on the back in a ponytail.

Michael didn't have any plans for this meeting, but looking back he had to admit that he never really had plans for their meetings. Theodorus ran the meetings and Michael just followed. He walked closer and shook Theodorus' hand firmly.

"I don't have much time left, Doc," Theodorus said in a rusty voice. Michael could see how fragile his body really was, thin pale arms covered with needle bruises from myriads of IVs in ICU, a thin neck with pronounced Adam's apple, deeply-seated eyes surrounded by dark circles. Michael's throat squeezed. Theodorus as always seemed to read his mind.

He smiled weakly, yet still somewhat mischievously. "It's okay. I am glad my time is coming. That was part of our deal, remember. You helped me to come closer to my privilege of leaving this world, Doc."

"You still have plenty of time left." Michael couldn't help his doctor's manner to reassure, but it sounded phony.

Theodorus' eyes retained the same all-knowing shining but there was deeper mystery in them now and he radiated new, deeper knowing, from beyond this world. Michael knew his reassurance was mostly for himself since Theodorus didn't need any.

"I am not afraid, you know, Doc. It's been a remarkable journey to spar with you, not like I would particularly miss your headquarters. No offense. Everything comes to its own conclusion. The art of it is in recognizing the right time for it. Not to be too impatient and not to miss the chance when your time comes. That can be applied to anything we humans do, you know."

Theodorus was speaking in riddles, as usual, and in generalizations, but this time Michael liked it because he understood that words were limited and often misleading.

There was no right or wrong way to say good-bye, and it felt comfortable for Michael to stand there and listen to what his patient had to say. He knew he wouldn't have another chance for this conversation.

Theodorus smiled and said, "The conversation will continue for those who are searching for answers, long after we change the place of our existence."

Michael shook his head and smiled back. "Before you draw me in your metaphors and generalizations, Mr. Theodorus, let me ask you something specific."

"By all means, Doc. I will tell you all I can."

"Why didn't you let the DA know the location of her last note? You know they wouldn't have even opened the case against you if they'd read it first."

"How do you know that I didn't?"

"Okay, so much for a promised straight answer."

"Did I promise a straight answer?" Theodorus laughed, obviously enjoying their dialogue. "Okay, okay, Doc, but if they knew right away that she was just leaving home, asking in her note not to look for her and not to worry about her, I might have missed my chance to meet such a refined psychiatrist as yourself. Think how much fun we would have missed."

Michael smiled again. All his hopes to get answers about the event that had taken place in the shack evaporated. Theodorus wasn't going to explain anything to him.

"I am not going to explain anything to you, Doc," Theodorus confirmed. He lifted his thin arm to his face and held it there as if preparing once again to wipe his nose. Instead, he smiled broadly, laughed at some joke only he understood, then pointed at Michael before dropping his arm to the wheelchair. "You will have plenty of time and experience to discover all the answers on your own. There is one thing I want to tell you, though. Consider it my parting gift, if you wish."

"You have my attention, Mr. Theodorus."

"Good. Let me tell you something about an important discovery that your fellow scientists are going to make in a couple of years." His half smile turned to a serious expression that looked like superiority, his sharp face portraying confidence that Michael never had seen on his face before.

Theodorus continued after a dramatic pause. "In a couple of years they are going to find out that the content of all this positive self-motivation talk, visualizing your success in the future, telling yourself that you are beautiful and loved and all this crap when your life is falling apart, is all meaningless nonsense, providing nothing more than steady income for self-help gurus. The content of the message that is sent to the brain doesn't matter. What matters is the repetition. I see you're getting it really fast, Doc."

He had obviously read the excitement that Michael felt as a surge went through his spine and goose bumps graced his flesh. He understood what Theodorus was talking about.

He continued, "Our brain responds to verbal commands no matter what they are, sad but true. The more we repeat something, the more solid the pathway for that message becomes until it is strong enough to compete with other pathways to take over behavior. You follow me? Sure you do. The problem with meaning is this: you can tell your face each morning when you look in the mirror how wonderful and happy and kind you are and how great your day is going to be, yet the running script for your day will come from myriads of unconscious repetitions telling you through fears and anxieties that have played out in your mind since childhood that you are a worthless loser and deserve nothing but suffering. This is how your day and your happiness will go down the toilet and the negative circle repeats itself again.

"So the problem is that the number of negative repetitions are way higher than any positive self-talk most people can produce. And the moment your fellow scientists realize this, they will come up with a bunch of stuff for regular folks that may start to really make a difference in their lives. The main focus will be in breaking the pattern of denial, for it is precisely the cover that allows all the negative programs to run free without checks and balances. What sounds almost like psycho-technical babble on the surface, deep down indicates the new direction of human evolution for which you, with your unusual experience, are a pioneer. You will be able to provide a lot of help for people in transition, something I know will make you really happy. You are the rarity behind these walls, you are a good doctor, Dr. Gate. Yet, I am sorry, I made a mistake, I called you a scientist. That, my friend, you are far from, and I mean that as a compliment. Your thinking is too multi-dimensional to conform to any linear science."

Michael laughed openly and loudly, with a true joy in his voice. "Thank you Mr. Theodorus. And I mean it. Thank you a lot."

Theodorus sighed. "I think the person is here to lead me where I am supposed to go. I am afraid it is good-bye, Dr. Gate." He smiled but his eyes looked genuinely sad.

Michael turned to see Lisa silently standing by the wall. He was surprised that he didn't hear her coming into the room. "Wow, Lisa you truly have skills to be invisible."

"I have learned from the best," she answered softly, but somewhat mischievously, and Michael laughed again remembering the story she'd told him, and how long ago, almost in another life, it seemed.

"Well, I have to follow the instructions of our young friend here as precisely as possible," said Theodorus as he awkwardly rolled his wheelchair toward Lisa. "Because she happens to be a great teacher, you know. She has been teaching me her Ba Gua meditations and, man, don't they come handy in my position."

Lisa smiled and started to roll his chair toward the door. "But before we can continue our Ba Gua lessons, Mr. Theodorus," she said, "I'm going to take you to the cafeteria, where you will have a specially prepared lunch from your super-restricted cardiac diet that I know you are extremely excited about."

Michael watched them leave. He felt sad but at peace. He nodded when Theodorus made a short circling movement with his hand, saying at the exit, "So long, Dr. Gate."

When the wheelchair was halfway out of the room, Theodorus turned back, looked at Michael and asked, "So what about Deniers Anonymous, Doc? I think it could be a really great idea."

Michael was momentarily speechless. *How could he know...?*

"You don't think you're the only one who shapeshifts, do you Doc?" Theodorus laughed softly, then turned to Lisa as they left the room, "I know, I know we absolutely can't be late for lunch."

Epilogue

The evening air was thick after the rain and it carried every smell straight to Michael's brain, bringing a wave of deep emotions to surface, layer after layer, as long-forgotten scents touched his nostrils with bursts of hot wind. His eyes were wet from tears or rain or both. He breathed heavily, taking in all the multitude of fragrances and sounds and colors that rushed toward him.

Michael licked his lips slowly. They had the cool, sweet taste of vanilla ice cream, exactly as he remembered it from his childhood. *Nice,* he said to himself and smiled as he kept walking through the city streets. He would remember every sweet sensation of this moment, every feeling, every sight, and every sound.

Nice.

Printed in Great Britain
by Amazon

41245412R00088